DEAR DIARY,

Christmas is my absolutely favorite holiday. I love singing carols, and there's nothing prettier than the glow of candles lighting everyone's windows. The meteorologists are notoriously inaccurate, but every day I check the forecast, hoping for snow.

Mom's always grumpy at Christmas, but this year is going to be different. Know why? Because I found Murphy O'Rourke.

He's fun and knows a lot of things and likes kids—I can tell. He'd be perfect for Mom, too. I don't know how I'm going to pull it off, but Mom and Murphy just have to get married. I really and truly want a father, and wouldn't it be great to get my own dad in time for Christmas?

Your friend,

Patty

Meet one of the seven winners of the American Romance Christmas Is For Kids Photo Contest, whose likeness appears on the cover of *Mrs. Scrooge*. She is Sarah Marie Mitchell of Regina, Saskatchewan. Her photo was entered by her grandmother, Enid D. Mitchell, who wrote to tell us of her granddaughter's delight in Christmas preparations.

What a "special" joy she is: Early on we look at Christmas catalogs; she decides on a Barbie Doll pool, from Grandma. At last the many packages are wrapped and under the tree—for Sarah, sister and cousins to pinch, shake and dream about. Then Christmas morning and opening time!

MRS. SCROOGE

BARBARA BRETTON

Harlequin Books

TORONTO • NEW YORK • LONDON
AMSTERDAM • PARIS • SYDNEY • HAMBURG
STOCKHOLM • ATHENS • TOKYO • MILAN

For Aunt Betty and Uncle Harry Miller,
who made the Christmas season so wonderful,
and for Mary Preisinger,
a friend for all seasons

Published December 1989

First printing October 1989

ISBN 0-373-16322-3

Chapter One

More than anything in the world ten-year-old Patricia Mary Elizabeth Dean wanted a father. Oh, she knew all about Ronald Donovan, the Air Force captain whose name was on her birth certificate, but except for a dim memory of a tall man with red hair just like hers, Ronald Donovan was nothing more than a biological fact.

Patty knew all about biological facts and how marriage and babies didn't always go hand in hand the way they did in old movies and television sitcoms. She'd heard stories about the days when a young girl had to leave home if she became pregnant out of wedlock but those days were long gone by the time it happened to her mother Samantha. Sam stayed right where she was, in her parents' house in Rocky Hill, and finished her senior year of high school. Nine months pregnant with Patty, she marched up to get her diploma then marched back out of the auditorium and headed for the hospital in Princeton. Five hours later Patty was born, and it seemed that from her very first breath Patty had been looking for a man to be her father.

It wasn't as if she was lonely or unloved or anything like that. She had her mom, Grandma Betty and Grandpa Harry, and enough aunts and uncles to make writing thank-you cards at Christmastime a real pain in the neck. And, of course, there were a pile of nosy neighbors and well-meaning friends who made sure Patty got home from school when she was supposed to and that Sam's beat-up old Blazer started up even on the coldest of winter days.

Patty was healthy, happy, and smart but she didn't have a father and that one fact made the other facts seem not very important at all. Her best friend Susan couldn't understand why Patty was so eager to have a father around the house. "My dad is always telling me I can't stay up to watch David Letterman," Susan complained just last week. "He won't let me wear nail polish or get a perm or even think about going to the movies with Bobby Andretti until I'm twenty-one. You're really a whole lot better off with just your mom, believe me."

Of course Patty didn't believe one single word of it. She knew she was meant to be part of a *real* family like the ones she saw on television. At night when she closed her eyes, she dreamed of Cliff Huxtable and Jason Seaver sitting at the head of the dining room table, carving the Christmas turkey while her mother proudly watched.

Not that Samantha Dean would ever just stand by and watch, mind you. Patty's mom was as independent and ambitious as they came. Sam had always managed to keep a roof over their heads and good food on the table, even while she juggled school work and taking care of Patty. The one thing Sam wasn't very good at was finding a man to be both husband and father, and so it was that Patty had decided to take over the quest.

And the moment Murphy O'Rourke walked into the room to give his career-day presentation, she knew her search was over.

Murphy O'Rourke wasn't handsome like a movie star, although his sandy brown hair was shiny and his hazel eyes held a friendly twinkle. He wore a brown polo shirt with a corduroy sport coat that was frayed at the elbows—and Patty couldn't imagine him sewing on those wimpy patches Susan's dad had on *his* corduroy sport coat.

He wasn't too short—probably stood just about six feet. He wasn't all pumped up like Arnold Schwarzenegger or real skinny like Woody Allen. He didn't have a fistful of gold rings or ugly puffs of chest hair sticking out of his shirt, and his voice didn't go all oily when he talked to grown-up women. When Mrs. Venturella introduced him to the class he didn't try to be funny or cool or any of the thousand other things that would have been the kiss of death as far as Patty was concerned.

He smiled at them as if they were real live people and said, "Good morning. I'm Murphy O'Rourke," and something inside Patty's heart popped like a birthday balloon.

"That's the one," she whispered to Susan. "He's perfect."

Susan's round gray eyes widened. *"Him?"* The girl looked down at the fact sheet in front of her. "He hasn't even been to college."

"I don't care. He's exactly what I've been looking for."

Susan wrinkled her nose. "He's old."

"So's my mother. That's what makes him so perfect."

"I liked the fireman," said Susan. "Did you see those muscles!" The girl sighed deeply and fluttered her eyelashes, and Patty could barely keep from hitting her best friend over the head with her math notebook.

"The fireman was stupid," said Patty. "He didn't even understand the theory behind water-pressure problems encountered fighting high-rise fires."

"Patty, *nobody* understands things like that except you."

"The nuclear physicist from Bell Labs understood."

"Then why don't you think he's the right man?"

"Because he called me 'little lady' when he answered my question on the feasibility of nuclear power near major urban centers."

"But he was cute," said Susan. "He had the most darling red suspenders and bow tie."

"I hate bow ties."

Susan made a face. "Oh, you hate everything, Patty Dean. I think you're about the snobbiest girl I've ever—"

"Patricia! Susan!" Mrs. Venturella rapped her knuckles sharply against the chalkboard at the front of the room. "If your conversation is so fascinating, perhaps, you'd be willing to share it with the rest of the class."

Susan's cheeks turned a bright red and she slumped down in her chair. "Sorry, Mrs. Venturella," she mumbled.

Patty found herself staring up at the twinkling hazel eyes of Murphy O'Rourke and suddenly unable to speak.

"Patricia," warned Mrs. Venturella. "Don't you have something to say?"

Murphy O'Rourke winked at her and before she knew it, the words came tumbling out. "Are you married?"

All around her the class was laughing but Patty didn't care. This was important.

O'Rourke looked her straight in the eye. "No, I'm not."

"Do you have any kids?"

"No. No kids."

"Do you—"

"That's enough, Patricia." Mrs. Venturella turned to O'Rourke and gave him one of those cute little "I'm sorry" shrugs Patty had seen the woman give Mr. MacMahon, the phys ed teacher with the hairy chest. "I apologize, Mr. O'Rourke. Patricia is one of our advanced students and she has an active curiosity."

"I make my living being curious," he said, then crossed his arms over his chest and leaned back against Mrs. Venturella's desk. He looked straight at Patty. "Go ahead. Ask me anything you want."

"On the *newspaper* business," said Mrs. Venturella, with a stern look for Patty, who still couldn't speak.

"Do you make a lot of money?" Craig Haley, class treasurer, asked.

"Enough to pay my rent," said O'Rourke.

"Did you ever go to China?" asked Sasha D'Amato.

"Twice." He grinned. "And I was thrown out once."

Danielle Meyer held up a copy of the *New York Telegram*. "How come I don't see your name anywhere?"

"Because I quit."

Patty was extremely impressed: he didn't so much as bat an eye when Mrs. Venturella gasped in horror.

"What do you do now?" Patty asked.

"I'm a bartender."

The only sound in the classroom was the pop of Susan's bubble gum.

"Look," he said, dragging his hand through his sandy brown hair, "I didn't mean to misrepresent anything. When you guys called and asked me to speak at the school, I was still a reporter for the *Telegram*. This is a pretty new development."

"Why'd you quit?" Patty asked. If there was anything her mom hated, it was a quitter. She hoped Murphy O'Rourke had a good reason for giving up a glamorous job as a New York City reporter and becoming a run-of-the-mill bartender, or it was all over.

"Artistic freedom," said Murphy O'Rourke.

"Bingo!" said Patty.

She'd finally found her man.

MURPHY O'ROURKE had faced hostile fire in Viet Nam in 1971. He had stared danger in the face everywhere from the subways of New York City to the back alleys of Hong Kong to the mean streets of Los Angeles and never broken into a sweat.

He'd been lied to, cursed at, beaten up and knocked down a time or two but he'd never—not ever—encountered anything like facing sixty curious New Jersey schoolkids on career day at Harborfields Elementary School in Montgomery Township.

All in all, it made running naked down the Turnpike backward in a blizzard seem like a day at the park.

They asked him about passports and phone taps. They asked him about deadlines and drug busts and protecting his sources. Those kids had more questions than the White House press corps and he had a hell of a time keeping up with them.

Why had he let his old man talk him into this, anyway? His father had always been big on community participation and had agreed to this command performance a few months before the massive heart attack that laid him low. When Murphy stepped in to take care of things for Bill, he hadn't expected his job description would include a visit to Sesame Street.

Funny how quickly it all came back to you with the first whiff of chalk dust. The pencils and the rulers; the big jars of library paste and gold stars for perfect attendance; blackboards and erasers and the unmistakable smell of wet boots on a snowy morning. Of course today there was also the hum of computers and the friendly LCD glow of hand-held calculators, but except for a few different trappings, it was still the same.

School.

Even though it had been over twenty-five years since he'd been in the fourth grade, he found that a few things never changed. It wasn't tough at all to peg that dark-haired boy in the first row as the class wiseguy, or the pretty little blonde near the window as the class flirt. The clown and the jock and most-likely-to-end-up-at-trade-school were just as easy to pick out.

But that serious-looking girl with the bright red hair and big blue eyes—damned if he could figure out where she fit in the scheme of things. She didn't ask the usual questions about the glamorous life of a reporter. Instead of giggling when he told his best "I interviewed Tom Cruise" story, she asked him if he'd ever been married. Hell, even after he told her he'd never taken the plunge, she went right ahead and asked him if he had kids, and she never so much as blushed. In fact she seemed more interested in knowing the details of his after-hours life than the details of his headline-making rescue of an Iranian hostage last year.

When Mrs. Venturella introduced the lawyer—"Anne Arvoti, divorce specialist"—Murphy breathed easily for the first time since he entered the classroom. He nodded at Mrs. Venturella, then was making a beeline toward the door when a small hand snaked out and grabbed him by the coat tails.

The red-haired girl with the ponytail. He should've known.

"You can't leave," she whispered, her freckled face earnest and eager. "There's a party afterward."

"I've got a bar to run," he whispered back, wondering why he felt like he'd been caught playing hooky and she was the truant officer.

"You have to stay," she insisted, clutching his coat more tightly. "I have to make sure that you—"

"Patty!" Mrs. Venturella's voice sounded to his right. "A bit more respect for Ms Arvoti's presentation, if you will."

He had to hand it to the kid. Her cheeks reddened but not for a second did she look away. "Please!" she mouthed, turning her head slightly so her teacher couldn't see. "You have to stay!"

Murphy hesitated. He hated schools. He hated school parties. He hated the thought of answering a thousand questions while he juggled milk and cookies and longed for a stiff Scotch. He had to get back to the bar and take over from Jack so the guy could grab himself some dinner. There was a meeting of the Tri-County Small Business Association at 7:00 p.m., then back to the bar for the usual late-night crowd. The last thing he had time for was playing Captain Kangaroo for a roomful of ten-year-olds.

But, damn it! This kid, Patty, was looking up at him with such unabashed eagerness that the rock that had passed for his heart for longer than he cared to remember thawed a bit.

"Christmas cookies, first of the season," she whispered, her blue eyes eager and bright behind her wire-rimmed glasses. "My mom made them."

"It's only December first," he whispered back. "Aren't you rushing things?"

"Christmas can't come soon enough for me, and, besides, I have a deal to offer you."

If there was one thing Murphy O'Rourke knew, it was when he had been bested. She was probably a Girl

Scout pushing chocolate mint cookies. He could handle that.

"Why not?" he said, shrugging his shoulders and taking a seat near the blackboard. One cup of milk, a few Santa Claus cookies, and he'd be out of there.

Another hour. What difference could one more hour possibly make?

IT TOOK MURPHY exactly fifteen minutes to find out.

The kid was some piece of work.

"Fifty dollars," Murphy said, meeting her fierce blue eyes. "Not a penny more."

"Sixty-five dollars a tray," Patty Dean stated in a voice Lee Iacocca would envy. "Anything less and we'd be running in the red."

Murphy threw his head back and laughed out loud. "I don't think you've ever run in the red in your life. You're one tough negotiator."

"Thank you." She didn't even blink. "But it will still be sixty-five dollars a tray. My mother is an expert chef, and food doesn't come cheap."

"Does your father have you on his payroll? You're better at this than most Harvard MBAs."

He caught the swift glitter of braces as a smile flickered across her freckled face. "My mother will be glad to hear that."

"And your dad?"

She shrugged her bony shoulders. "I wouldn't know. The last time I saw him I was two years old."

"Two?"

"Yes," she said. "My long-term memory is excellent and I remember him quite clearly."

Murphy wouldn't have thought it possible but his battle-scarred heart again showed signs of life. He'd grown up without his mother, and he knew that the emptiness never left, no matter how old you got or how successful. "Yeah, well, then tell your mom she has one hell of a businesswoman on her hands."

"Sixty-two fifty," Patty said. "Take it or leave it."

"Sixty-three," said Murphy, extending his right hand and engulfing the girl's hand in his. "Not a penny less."

Patty's auburn brows rose above the tops of her eyeglasses. "Sixty-three? Are you certain?"

"Take it or leave it."

"You're got yourself a deal, Mr. O'Rourke."

Patty gave him her mother's business card and promised that Samantha Dean would be at the Tri-County meeting later that evening to finalize the arrangements. Feeling smug and self-satisfied, Murphy grabbed an extra cookie and headed out toward his car in the rainswept parking lot.

It wasn't until he was halfway back to the bar that he realized he'd just made a deal with a ten-year-old budding corporate shark whose mother might take a dim view of handshake agreements with unemployed gonzo journalists who were now pulling drafts for a living.

And, all things considered, he wouldn't blame her one bit.

SAMANTHA DEAN stifled a yawn as the New Jersey Transit train rumbled toward the station at Princeton Junction. The railroad car was cold and damp and it took every ounce of imagination in Sam's body to conjure up visions of hot soup and a roaring fire. Before she knew it she'd be home with Patty, the two of them snug in their favorite robes as they watched *MacGyver* and *Monday Night Football*.

"One more day," she said to her best friend Caroline. "Twenty-four hours and I never have to ride this blasted cattle car again."

"Speak for yourself," said Caroline, eyeing the handsome businessmen sitting opposite the two women. "I rather enjoy riding the train."

Sam resisted the urge to kick Caroline in her fashionable ankle. "You wouldn't mind a trek through the Sahara if there was a man involved."

"Try it some time," Caroline said, her dimples deepening. "You might find you like it. Men are pleasant creatures, once you tame them."

I'd rather tame a grizzly bear, Sam thought. At least grizzly bears hibernated six months of every year. She could never find time in her crazy daily schedule for a man, no matter how handsome. She turned and looked at her fluffy blond friend. "Do me a favor," she said, giving way to another yawn. "Why don't we just pretend you gave me matchmaking lecture number 378 and be done with it?" Caroline started to protest but Sam raised a hand to stop her. "It's not as if I haven't heard it all before."

Caroline leaned her head against the worn leather seat. Even at the end of a rainy, cold Monday she looked superb. If they weren't best friends, Sam just might hate the woman.

"You may think you've heard it all," Caroline said, "but I can tell you haven't paid attention. Patty needs a father, Sam."

Sam's jaw settled into a stubborn line. "Patty has a father," she snapped. "It's not my fault Ronald doesn't care that he has a daughter."

Caroline was as stubborn as Sam. "I'm not talking about Ronald Donovan and you know it. I'm talking about you, Sam. About your future."

"My future is fine, thank you. This time next month, I'll be open for business and from there the sky's the limit." For two years Sam had eaten, breathed, slept Fast Foods for the Fast Lane and she was finally on the eve of reaping the benefits of her backbreaking schedule of work and school and motherhood.

"There's more to life than your career, Sam."

"Easy for you to say. You have a career. Mine hasn't started yet."

"There's Patty," Caroline said softly, tearing her limpid blue-eyed gaze away from the man in the gray flannel suit across the aisle. "You should think about her happiness."

Sam's fatigue disappeared in a quick blaze of anger. "That's exactly what I'm thinking about, Caroline. Patty needs more than I could ever give her by waiting tables or typing envelopes. Fast Foods for the Fast Lane is my best hope."

Having a genius for a daughter wasn't your everyday occurrence. As it was, Patty was quickly outstripping the ability of Harborfields Elementary School to keep up with her. Unfortunately Patty's nimble mind was also quickly outstripping Sam's financial ability to provide tutors, books, and advanced courses her little girl deserved but didn't have.

Sam had no college degree, no inheritance to fall back upon, no friends in high places. What she had was a sharp mind, common sense, and the ability to turn the simplest of foods into the most extraordinary fare. With the area around Princeton booming with two-paycheck families and upscale life-styles, Sam realized that all the modern conveniences in the world couldn't compensate for the lack of a home-cooked meal made to order and ready when you were.

From that simple idea came her brainchild, Fast Foods for the Fast Lane, and with it the hope that she would be able to give Patty every chance in the world to achieve her potential.

The tinny voice of the conductor blared from the loudspeaker: "Princeton Junction, next stop!"

Caroline, elegant as always in her timeless gray silk dress, stood up and reached for her parcels in the overhead rack. "I should be imprisoned for grand larceny," she said, sitting back down next to Sam, her lap piled high with loot. "Three Bob Mackie beaded beauties and a Donna Karan business special and I didn't have to empty my bank account."

"I take it business is going well?" Sam asked, collecting her books and papers from the empty seat next to her. Caroline ran an offbeat boutique called Twice Over Lightly, where one-of-a-kind designer dresses could be rented for a night by New Jersey Cinderellas.

Caroline's broad smile told the tale. "It's going so well I can afford to wear the Schiaparelli to the Tri-County Masquerade Ball. Jeannie Tremont will be green with envy."

"No," said Sam, searching her briefcase for her car keys. "Absolutely not."

"Absolutely not what?" Caroline asked.

"I am absolutely *not* going to the Christmas party."

"Of course you are," Caroline said. "Don't be silly."

"I hate Christmas parties and I refuse to go to one where all the adults wear Santa Claus masks. I have better things to do with my free time." *Like eating, sleeping, and being Patty's mother.*

Caroline's elegant nose wrinkled in disdain. "Spare me your Mrs. Scrooge routine, Sam. It was old last year."

"I don't ask you to forgo your mistletoe, Caroline," Sam said evenly. "Don't go asking me to run around whistling 'Jingle Bells.'"

"You used to love Christmas," Caroline persisted. "You used to start decorating before Thanksgiving."

"I used to wear braids and watch *Leave It to Beaver*, too."

"You even celebrated Christmas the year you were expecting Patty and we both know what a rotten holiday that was. She's still waiting to set up the luminaria along the driveway on Christmas Eve."

"I was seventeen." Had there ever been a time when setting up those tiny white candles outside had seemed so wondrous, so important? "I didn't know any better."

Leave it to Samantha Dean to fall in love with a boy from the right side of the tracks. A high school romance with a girl from Rocky Hill was one thing; marriage to that very same girl was something else entirely.

There would be no marriage, said the illustrious Donovan clan, not even to legitimize the baby Sam carried. And so it was on Christmas Eve that Ronald was whisked away from the temptation and sent west where he ended up in the United States Air Force Academy, on the road to a bright and shiny future as a pilot.

And good riddance.

Sam had done fine by Patty up until now and, God willing, she would do even better once her catering business got rolling.

"You should get out more," Caroline continued, as the train rattled into the station. "Socialize. Christmas soirees are all part of doing business in this town, Sam."

"Well, the soirees will have to go on without me. I have ten weeks' worth of work and only four weeks to accomplish it. Believe me, I don't have time for Christmas."

"Everyone has time for Christmas."

Sam laughed out loud. "You don't even have time for the Tri-County meeting tonight."

"That's different. The store is open tonight and Jeannie has the evening off." She narrowed her eyes in Sam's direction. "I hope you're going."

Sam glanced out at the cold rain lashing against the train windows. "Not me. I intend to stretch out on the sofa and watch *Taxi* reruns while Patty tackles nuclear fusion."

"Not a very businesslike attitude, Sam."

"I'm not in business yet, Caroline."

Caroline waved her words away. "A mere technicality. You should be out there spreading Christmas cheer. I don't think you're being fair to Patty." Caroline looked altogether too pleased with her logic for Sam's taste.

"Just because I don't turn all warm and mushy when I hear 'Deck the Halls,' doesn't mean I'm going to deny Patty her fun."

"Well, thank God for that," Caroline murmured. "I would have kidnaped that girl for the holidays."

"Wait until I'm established," Sam said. "In a few years I'll have plenty of time for Christmas celebrations."

"I certainly hope so. Christmas is a time for miracles, honey, and there are few of them around these days. Who knows? Your big break might be waiting for you at the Tri-County meeting." Caroline patted Sam's hand. "You just have to believe."

"Oh, I believe," said Sam as the train stopped and the doors slid open. "I believe in peace on earth, joy to the world, and that not even Tom Selleck could tempt me to go to that meeting tonight."

Chapter Two

"No," Sam said, kicking off her wet Reeboks and collapsing into a kitchen chair. She'd been home less than fifteen minutes and already Patty was trying to push her back out the door. "Absolutely not."

Her daughter's bright blue eyes flashed with a spark of stubborn recklessness that Sam was all too familiar with. Nothing short of a world-class brainstorm would have kept Patty away from Monday-afternoon Math Club.

"But, Mom, I—"

Sam groaned and closed her eyes. "Not another word, kiddo. The only place I'm going tonight is to bed."

Patty's cheeks flushed with determination. "I promised you'd go to the meeting."

Wearily Sam braced herself and opened one dark brown eye. "That's what you get for making promises you can't keep."

"You have to go! I'll be humiliated if you don't."

"Then prepare yourself to be humiliated, Patty, because I'm not moving from this house." She stifled a yawn. "I may not even move from this chair."

"That's very unprofessional, Mother."

So it's going to be one of those nights, is it? Whenever Patty called Sam "Mother," Sam knew she was in for trouble.

"How can you be a small business when you don't go to small-business meetings?" her small and brilliant daughter reasoned.

"I'm not a small business yet, kiddo, and I never will be if I don't finish this last course." Loss Management and Customer Relations had turned out to be a combination of Abnormal Psychology 101 and Deficit Spending for the Soon-to-be-Bankrupt, while Food Preparation and You made Martha Stewart's elaborate arrangements look like leftovers. "What I need is warm food, a hot bath and a good night's sleep."

Patty's red brows knotted together over the bridge of her eyeglasses. "Test tomorrow?"

"A final."

"Scared?"

Sam opened her other eye. "What is this—*Invasion of the Body Snatchers*? You're the ten-year-old. You should be the one taking tests and I should be the one looking concerned."

Patty grinned and lifted the lid on Sam's favorite saucepan and the mouthwatering aroma of chili filled the tiny kitchen.

"I even left out the garlic," Patty said.

Sam had been a mother long enough to recognize a con job when she saw one, but there was something so wonderful about hot chili on a cold, wet evening that her maternal defense mechanism lowered.

"Did you remember to brown the meat?" Sam asked, weakening.

"Of course!" Her oh-so-grown-up little girl looked highly affronted. "And I mixed my own chili powder instead of using the bottled stuff."

Sam sighed. Although she prided herself on her Cordon Bleu-style of cooking, chili was her downfall and Patti knew it. "The spirit is willing," Sam muttered, "but the flesh is *very* weak. What's the catch, kiddo?"

Patty was the picture of innocence. "There's no catch."

"Patty." Sam's voice was stern as she struggled to hide her grin. Despite her genius IQ, Patty was transparent as plate glass, a fact for which Sam was forever grateful. It was one of the few advantages she had left. "You didn't volunteer me for another Christmas Party committee at school, did you?"

"I wouldn't dare," Patty said. "Not after the kids nicknamed you Mrs. Scrooge last year." Patty ladled some chili into a heavy white bowl and handed it to Sam. "I just think you should go to the meeting tonight, that's all."

The chili was warm, spicy, and downright delicious and Sam's defenses lowered yet another notch. "Any particular reason?"

Patty met her eyes head-on. "I think it's good business."

"What's his name?"

"Maa—aa! Why are you being so suspicious?"

"Because I'm a mother, that's why. The chili is terrific, kiddo, and I'm probably going to go to the darned meeting tonight but I think I deserve a straight answer, don't you?"

"Murphy O'Rourke," said Patty, sitting down at the table opposite Sam with her own steaming bowl of chili.

"What?"

"His name. Murphy O'Rourke."

"Oh, Patty!" Sam's spoon clattered back into the heavy white bowl. "You know how I feel about matchmaking. I don't have enough time for you much less a boyfriend."

"I'm not matchmaking," her daughter protested. "This is a business matter."

"You're making me nervous, Patty."

"He runs a bar in Rocky Hill and he lost his chef. I told him you could supply the food for the bar until he hires a new chef."

"Cook, honey. Bars don't have chefs." There was something very daunting about a ten-year-old child with the instincts of a Donald Trump. "I suppose you also negotiated a price."

She had. Sam whistled low. "That much?"

Patty nodded. "I probably could have asked fifty percent more but it's Christmastime."

"What does Christmas have to do with good business?"

"Really, Mother!"

"Oh, don't look so shocked, honey. I was only kidding." Each year she vowed to make an effort for Patty's sake, and each year it grew harder and harder to do. "How much did you say the job would pay?"

Patty told her again.

It was still impressive.

"And you wouldn't even have to work there," Patty continued, her voice eager. "You could make up the food here and drop it off at the bar on your way to the train."

"And school finishes up tomorrow," Sam said, warming to the idea despite her better judgment. With that amount of money for making a few hors d'oeuvres for a local tavern, she'd have time to get the store ready for its opening day, sleep late, Christmas shop and be able to pay her bills. It was too good to pass up. "What time did you say the meeting was?"

"Eight o'clock," said Patty, her small freckled face beaming with excitement.

"And he'll be there?"

Her daughter's red braids bounced as she nodded her head. "Yes. He promised to give you first chance at the job."

"All right," said Sam, giving in at last. "I'll go. If I'm going to be the Princeton corridor's number one entrepreneur, I suppose I'd better start entrepreneuring."

Patty leaped up and nearly vaulted the kitchen table in order to envelope her mother in a bear hug.

"You're the best mother in the world!" the little girl exclaimed in delight. "The absolute best!"

TWO HOURS LATER, the best mother in the world stood in the doorway of the meeting room and took stock of the crowd. Brooks Brothers, Savile Row, and a touch of the Talbot's catalog thrown in for good measure. Ivy League personified.

She glanced down at her flour-speckled sweater and trusty cords. Whatever had possessed her to be so cavalier about the Tri-County Small Business Association anyway? An elegantly coiffed woman in a navy suit and red shirt walked by with a nod of her head and instantly Sam felt two feet tall.

Eye shadow, thought Sam with a groan. *Gold earrings and lipstick and a clean sweater and that's just for starters.* Everything Patty had begged and pleaded for Sam to wear. As it was, she looked like a holdover from the Sixties. All she needed was a peace symbol embroidered on her pants pocket, love beads around her neck and a picket sign proclaiming her disdain for all things material.

Maybe she should pretend she was there to scrub the floors in the ladies' room. Judging by her appearance, that would be an easier sell than trying to convince these tailored wonders that she was one of them.

She stepped inside the doorway, keeping the wall firmly against her back. Where on earth had she gotten the idea that these meetings were casual? Well, there was no hope for it. Sam hadn't come all that way to slink out of there without accomplishing her objective. Sixty-three dollars for a tray of cocktail sandwiches wasn't something she could easily turn away from and, like it or not, Mr. Murphy O'Rourke would have to accept her the way she was or find someone else to do business with.

She eased into the crowd and scanned the stick-on name tags affixed to bosoms and pecs, feeling vaguely like an upscale pervert. Kaplan...Oliveri... DeSoto...Brennan... Everything but O'Rourke.

A tall, dark and handsome man in a sophisticated tweed suit approached. If this was Patty's business conquest, she would have to compliment her daughter on her good taste. He was positively gorgeous.

"Good evening," he said, white teeth gleaming.

Sam straightened her shoulders and wished she'd at least worn her hair down instead of in a ponytail. "Good evening."

"Still cold outside?"

"Freezing, but at least it isn't snowing."

Nodding, he drained a styrofoam cup of coffee. "The pot's empty."

"I beg your pardon?"

"The coffeepot's empty," he repeated. "I believe we could use more. The meeting's about to begin."

Sam arched a brow. "Then perhaps you should speak to someone who might be able to help you."

He had the decency to flush beneath his perfect tan. "I thought—I mean, aren't you—"

"No, I'm not."

His dark blue eyes traveled swiftly over her bedraggled form and she held her breath, praying he wouldn't call a security guard to evict her from the premises.

"I'm waiting for someone," she said, although it was really none of his business. "I *am* a member."

"I'm sure," he said, nodding, but it was obvious he had difficulty imagining an overaged street urchin being granted membership in such a hallowed institution.

Might as well go for broke, Sam. "You wouldn't happen to be Murphy O'Rourke, would you?"

"Afraid not," he murmured in a lock-jawed parody of all things Ivy then moved back into the crowd.

We need to have a long *talk, Patty,* she thought as she poured herself a tall glass of iced water and watched the Ralph Lauren sweaters mingle with the Laura Ashley dresses.

"Quite a turnout, isn't it?" asked a middle-aged man in aviator glasses.

"Quite," said Sam, feigning an air of privileged indifference. There were far too many prep school clothes at the Tri-County meeting for her taste. She'd spent a good part of her early adult life feeling second place to people whose claim to superiority was nothing more profound than being born in the right zip code.

Come on, O'Rourke, she thought, returning to her place by the double doors. She wanted to meet the man, solidify Patty's deal, and go home—preferably in the next five minutes, if possible. She scanned the smoke-filled room once again. Sam had checked the name tag of every man who even remotely matched her daughter's description of the elusive Murphy O'Rourke to no avail. In fact, not one of the men she'd approached had even heard of O'Rourke. Either Patty was playing an extremely unfunny practical joke or the mystery man had been stringing along a little girl who had been known to get more-than-a-little pushy when she was trying to make a point.

One day when Fast Foods for the Fast Lane was underway she would belong here with the Stocktons and the Witherspoons and the Donovans, but this definitely wasn't the day. She was cold and wet and exhausted and positive she should have stayed home with a blanket and a hot-water bottle as she'd originally planned.

A white-haired woman took the podium, rapped sharply with her gavel, then launched into a series of public address announcements with a delivery flat as the Mojave Desert.

"Oh, no," muttered a male voice behind Sam. "I should've stayed home and watched the game."

A kindred spirit! Who would have imagined it possible? Eagerly she spun around in time to see a scruffy man in a battered trench coat blow into the room with all the grace and charm of the north wind. His black umbrella was inside out, his hair was wet and plastered to his forehead, and he was mumbling words not often heard in the environs of Princeton. Sam was surprised they'd let him in without fingerprinting him.

"Hold this," he said, pushing the cockeyed umbrella and a soggy sheaf of papers into her hands. "Damn coat's soaked."

Sam stared down at the umbrella and papers in shock. "Hold them yourself," she said, pushing them back at him.

"Come on," he said, his sandy hair dripping water into his hazel eyes. "Just let me hang the coat over the radiator and I'll take everything off your hands."

"You'll take everything off my hands *now*," said Sam, in the same tone of voice she used on Patty.

"Full of Christmas spirit, aren't you, lady?" he mumbled, but Sam noted he retrieved his belongings quickly enough.

"I suppose Christmastime is an excuse for bad manners these days." Who did this scruffy barbarian think he was, anyway? She owed Caroline an apology. Apparently there really was something to be said for dressing for success; she hadn't worked this hard and this long to be mistaken for a hatcheck girl.

He was grumbling under his breath about feeling like a circus juggler, and Sam turned to find another spot to wait for Murphy O'Rourke when a terrible thought struck her. Ridiculous. That scruffy looking specimen couldn't possibly be Patty's new business partner. Patty had described a tall and handsome man with money to burn. She took another look at the man in the worn corduroy jacket. Certainly no one would call him handsome. Attractive, maybe, in a somewhat battered kind of way with his large-boned build and the rugged face that had taken a punch or two in its day, but not even Patty could describe him as a hunk.

And as for looking like the proper Princetonian businessman—well, he had none of the sheen and polish of the men at the Tri-County meeting. No perfectly barbered coif for this man; his hair tickled his collar and flopped over his ears and looked as if it hadn't seen a stylist's scissors in a very long time.

But then, the man Patty had struck a deal with owned a bar not a barrister's office and this man looked exactly the way Sam imagined a saloon keeper should look.

And let's face facts, Sam, she thought as he met her eyes and flashed her a roguish grin. This was exactly the type of man Patty would think just terrific.

He appeared at Sam's elbow. "Any seats available or are you planning on a quick getaway?"

Sam gestured toward an empty row near the podium. "Be my guest. I'm waiting for someone."

"So am I."

That's what I was afraid of. She turned and looked up at him. "Murphy O'Rourke?"

He nodded. "Samantha Dean?"

She extended her hand. "I believe you and my daughter arranged a business deal today."

His grip was firm without being macho. A pleasant surprise. "The kid's sharp," he said, grinning. "I wouldn't want to face her at an arbitration table."

A man in the last row turned around and loudly shushed them.

"Look," Sam whispered, spirits sinking, "I don't think business deals made by a ten-year-old are binding. If you want out, I'll—"

The entire last row swiveled to glare at Sam and Murphy O'Rourke. Chastened, they found seats near the window and Sam struggled to stay awake during an interminable discussion of the Holiday Ball next Saturday night.

"If I snore, kick me," O'Rourke ordered, then closed his eyes.

Sam almost fell off her folding chair in surprise. All around them the most ambitious entrepreneurs in the region were exchanging business cards, setting up power breakfasts, and deciding whether the main arboreal theme for the masquerade ball should be mistletoe or holly. The air bristled with energy and, at least when they weren't discussing the Christmas party, Sam found herself itching for January first to roll around so she could be a real part of things.

Not O'Rourke. He was slumped in his chair, arms folded across his chest, head thrown back as if he didn't give a fig what any of Princeton's best and brightest thought about him. Sam was torn between admiration and horror. She had a healthy respect for clubs and associations and institutions, mainly because they had always seemed just beyond her grasp.

"All in favor of holly in the ballroom and mistletoe in the anterooms, signify by saying aye."

A chorus of *ayes* rang out. Sam withheld her opinion on general principle since she wouldn't be an official entrepreneur for another four weeks. Next to her, O'Rourke made a noise like a strangled moose.

"Ouch!" He leaned forward and rubbed his left ankle. "What the hell was that all about?"

"You snored," Sam said. "I'm saving you the embarrassment of public disgrace."

He inclined his head toward the podium. "Do you care about the dinner menu for the Christmas dance?"

"No."

"The wine list?"

"Not one bit."

His sleepy hazel eyes narrowed as he met hers. "How do you feel about the Giants?"

"True love," she said. "If you're a Jets fan, the deal's off."

"Mention the Jets at O'Rourke's and you buy drinks for the house."

"An admirable policy."

"How would you feel about ironing out our deal at the bar while we watch the game?"

He may not be a candidate for the cover of *GQ*, but Murphy O'Rourke was a man after her own heart. At least, in the business sense. "If we hurry, we might catch the end of the second quarter."

"You're okay, Samantha Dean," he said, flashing a devilish grin. "Let's go."

THE LOOK on Aunt Caroline's face was even better than a gift subscription to *Science Digest*.

"You've done the impossible," Caroline breathed, lowering herself into the rocking chair near the stereo.

"I know," said Patty, beaming with delight, as she handed Caroline a cup of hot tea then curled up on the sofa.

"The one meeting I skip and you convince your mother to go. How did you do it—hypnosis?"

"Money," said Patty proudly.

Caroline's perfectly lipsticked mouth dropped open. "You bribed your own mother? What kind of allowance do you get, girl?"

"I cut Mom a business deal."

"That does it," said Caroline, laughing. "Would you be my business manager, too?"

Patty felt happier than she had the day she won the Mid-Atlantic Science Fair with her work on water purification. Aunt Caroline wasn't one of those grown-ups who fell all over kids, pouring on the praise as if it was maple syrup. A compliment from her always had Patty walking on air for days.

Caroline listened closely as Patty told all about Career Day and Murphy O'Rourke and the saga of the sixty-three-dollar trays of food.

"And Mom couldn't resist," Patty finished up, her voice triumphant.

"Okay, Ms Trump," said Caroline, leaning forward, "what's the catch?"

Patty felt her cheeks redden beneath the woman's knowing gaze. "There's no catch."

"Of course there's a catch."

Patty looked down at her feet which were stuffed into humongous bunny slippers. "Okay, so maybe I do have an ulterior motive," Patty said finally.

"Matchmaking again?" Her aunt shivered delicately. "You like to live dangerously, Patricia."

Patricia! How grown-up that sounded. How sophisticated. Leave it to Aunt Caroline to think of something so wonderful.

"You matchmake," Patty said, wishing she were wearing normal slippers. It was hard to be adult when your feet looked like Bugs Bunny. "Mom says that's all you ever have on your mind."

"Out of the mouths of babes," muttered Caroline, smoothing one pale brow with a manicured fingertip. "So what is he like?"

"Wonderful!" said Patty, forgetting that she was feeling sophisticated and worldly. "Perfect!" Just the thought of Murphy O'Rourke was enough to make Patty feel all Christmasy and happy inside, like the first snowfall of the season.

Caroline's blue eyes twinkled with delight. "I suppose he's handsome?"

For a second Patty couldn't conjure up a face to go with her romantic notions. "He's very . . . manly."

"Handsome?" Caroline repeated.

"Not exactly," said Patty as his image clarified. "He's kind of rugged."

"Uh-oh," said Caroline. "That bad, is he?"

"He's not bad at all," Patty said, leaping to his defense. She had an IQ in the top .05% percentile in the nation. Why couldn't she find the words to tell Caroline about the man she was certain would one day be her dad? "He was a foreign correspondent."

"I thought you said he owned a bar."

"He does now but he used to be a reporter."

"Does he look like he needs a shave?"

Patty nodded. "Five o'clock shadow."

"And he smokes?"

She thought about the pack of cigarettes tucked in his shirt pocket and the matches he'd cadged from Mrs. Venturella. "Camels."

"Last question," said Caroline, "and this one will tell the whole story—does he wear a trench coat?"

Patty's heart pounded wildly inside her chest. "An old one," she said, "and no hat." Murphy O'Rourke was the kind of man who laughed at the elements. In her wildest imagination she couldn't picture him as a little boy, all bundled up in galoshes and muffler and rain hat.

Caroline leaned back in the rocking chair and fixed Patty with a look. "Poor old Sam," she said, starting to laugh. "The girl doesn't stand a chance!"

Chapter Three

O'Rourke's Bar and Grill looked exactly the way a tavern in central New Jersey should look, and the moment Sam stepped inside, she felt at home. O'Rourke's boasted a great deal of gleaming mahogany, shiny brass, and enough beer mugs to keep the crew on *Cheers* happy for another eight seasons. A group of men well over voting age were clustered around a table near the old juke box, arguing loudly over great baseball teams of the past, while the football Giants played their hearts out on the big-screen TV mounted overhead.

The air smelled pleasantly of pipe tobacco, Old Spice and spirits, and Sam couldn't help but smile at the dark-haired waitress who scurried by, carrying a pitcher of beer and six glasses to the over-the-hill gang at the table. No hanging ferns and Perrier at this bar.

She peered around at the other customers. There also were no women. This was obviously that most sacrosanct of male establishments—the local watering hole—and she made a mental note to forget the watercress sandwiches on crustless pumpernickel in favor of ham and cheese on rye.

"Hang your coat on the rack by the door," O'Rourke said. "I'll get you a draft."

"Make it a hot chocolate and you're on."

The silence in the tavern was daunting as she strolled over to the coatrack. Murphy, the dark-haired waitress, and the Over-the-Hill-Gang all watched her as if she were a land mine.

"Hot chocolate?" Murphy O'Rourke sounded incredulous. "How about an Irish coffee?"

"I'm driving," said Sam. "Hot chocolate will be fine."

Murphy vaulted over the bar and rummaged noisily beneath the counter. "I don't see any hot chocolate back here."

The cluster of senior citizens found that highly amusing and they laughed along with O'Rourke.

Sam called up her friendliest smile. "How about a cup of coffee, then?"

"I don't think we have any," said Murphy, looking oddly uncomfortable behind the bar.

The waitress hit him on the arm with her tray. "Idiot! You can't make Irish Coffee without it, can you?"

His grin was sheepish. "I didn't think of that."

Not good, thought Sam. A saloon owner who didn't know the first thing about something as basic as Irish Coffee—and a saloon owner named O'Rourke, at that. No wonder he fell for Patty's spiel. He motioned for Sam to take a seat and she was about to claim a bar stool when the most elegant of golden agers rose to his feet and executed a courtly bow.

"We'd be honored if you joined us," he said.

"I'd love to," said Sam, glancing at O'Rourke who was still rattling around with the coffee pot, "but we have business to discuss."

"We have known Murphy since he was in knee pants. There is no business he cannot discuss in our presence."

Who would have figured the mercurial, devil-may-care man she'd met at the Tri-County meeting to be a part of a most intriguing extended family? She had to hand it to Patty; her daughter rarely befriended anyone ordinary.

"Forget it, Scotty." Murphy vaulted the bar once again then picked up two cups of coffee. "She's too young for you."

"Age is a state of mind," the older man pronounced in the lofty tones of a Princeton professor, "and I am in my prime."

His peers broke into hoots of laughter and a few clumsy, but amiable, jokes about snow on the roof and a fire in the furnace.

"Ignore them," said O'Rourke, leading Sam to a table on the other side of the room. "It's past their bedtime."

"Respect!" boomed the gentleman he'd called Scotty. "We are the only buffer between this establishment and bankruptcy court, my boy."

Sam's eyes widened. "Business isn't good?" *And you're willing to pay over sixty bucks a tray for sandwiches?*

"Business is booming," he said, sitting down opposite her, "but they still like to think they're the cornerstone of the bar."

Scotty winked at Sam and she chuckled. "Why is it I think they probably are?"

"You're a lot like your kid," said O'Rourke. "Blunt."

Sam nodded. "To a fault. It's a family trait."

He took a gulp of coffee then gestured broadly. "So what do you think of the place?"

"I think it's terrific. I didn't think bars like this existed anymore."

"They don't," said Murphy. "The fern bars are taking over the world."

The thought of ferns overtaking O'Rourke's made Sam laugh out loud. "A fern would choke on the cigar smoke in this place."

"Does it bother you?" he asked.

"Not a bit." Even if it did, she wouldn't have said so. Sam was blunt but she understood the rules. Everything about O'Rourke's was exactly as it should be—including the shroud of smoke settling over her shoulders. She gestured toward the old boxing photos on the brick wall next to her. "That's Joe Louis, isn't it?"

"My dad's a fight fan. You should see how many boxes of memorabilia he has stuffed in his attic."

She took a sip of the hot, surprisingly good, coffee. "It's nice of you to hang some of them up. Gives the place atmosphere."

"My dad'll be glad to hear that." He met her eyes. "It's his bar."

"What?" She couldn't keep her surprise from her voice.

"It's his bar," O'Rourke repeated. "I'm babysitting until he's back on his feet."

She leaned closer, her curiosity piqued. "What happened to him?"

"Heart attack." O'Rourke's voice lowered and he looked away for a split second. Just long enough for Sam to see both fear and love in his hazel eyes. "Guy doesn't even smoke."

"How is he? My uncle had a heart attack two years ago and he's back out there running eight miles a day."

"Pop's more the recliner-chair-and-remote-control type, but he's almost one hundred percent."

"And you're the resident barkeep?"

O'Rourke raked his shaggy brown hair off his forehead and grinned. "I can pull a draft with the best of 'em. Just don't go getting fancy on me."

The thought of Murphy O'Rourke fixing a piña colada, complete with the pineapple spear and paper parasol, was comical. "Judging by your clientele, you're safe. They look like a sturdy, all-American brew crowd to me."

"Does that disappoint you?"

Sam's eyes widened and she looked down at her baggy sweater and cords. "Do I look like the Perrier-and-lime type to you?"

"No," he said, that smile of his back in place. "That's one of the things I like about you."

Sam listened while he told her about the long recovery period Bill O'Rourke was going through. Murphy's brother in Florida had tried to convince Bill to put the tavern up for sale but the older man was adamant that it stay open, even if a stranger had to come in and tend to things in his absence.

"And you put aside your own career to come take care of things for your dad?" Sam couldn't keep the admiration from her voice as visions of *Happy Days* and Richie Cunningham helping out at the family hardware store spun through her head. "I'm impressed."

O'Rourke grunted and downed his coffee. "Before you nominate me for the *Croix de Guerre*, I should tell you there wasn't any career to put aside. I've been unemployed for the past few months."

She instantly understood the worn elbows on his corduroy jacket and the deplorable condition of his raincoat. Poor man was down on his luck and probably thrilled to have a steady job to go to each morning. "A strike?"

"In a manner of speaking." His hazel eyes glittered with a challenge as he met her gaze straight on. "Actually I walked out."

"Out of what?" It wasn't difficult to imagine him staging a walkout at a steel mill or an automobile assembly plant. He looked like the kind of man who wasn't afraid of hard work. Unfashionable work that dirtied your clothes and blackened your hands.

"I walked out of the New York office of the *Telegram*."

She sprayed coffee clear across the table and onto the lapels of his sorry excuse for a jacket. "Very funny. You had me going there for a moment."

"I'm not joking. I was managing editor."

Sam had a sense of humor. She could go along with the joke. "And I suppose before that you were foreign correspondent for Reuters."

"AP," he said. "First Moscow, then London."

"You should be a writer, O'Rourke. You have a way with fiction."

"I *am* a writer but I deal with the facts."

"Being a bartender is nothing to be ashamed of."

"If I were a bartender I wouldn't be ashamed."

"Okay," said Sam, mopping up the spill with a cocktail napkin. "Have it your way. Let's talk about the sandwich trays."

"I'm not kidding, Samantha."

"I said I believed you, O'Rourke." She whipped a notepad out of her pocketbook and uncapped a felt tip pen. "Do you want heros or club sandwiches?"

"Heros." He gulped more coffee. "I walked out on the paper as a protest for artistic freedom."

"Turkey, ham, or tuna salad?"

"Aren't you listening to a damn thing I'm saying?" He glared at her. "I thought club sandwiches were usually B.L.T.s."

"Good tomatoes are out of season. How about roast beef?"

"Jeez..." He dragged a hand through his shaggy, still-damp hair. "Some of each, why don't you?"

Sam scribbled a few lines then looked back up. "With lettuce? Without lettuce? Pickles? Assorted condiments? Perhaps a side of cole slaw and—"

"Gimme a break, will you?" He yanked the pen from her hand. "I don't care if you make peanut butter and jelly sandwiches."

Her eyebrows arched. "At sixty-three dollars a tray, I'd make quite a profit." He couldn't be a businessman by profession because he would have run himself into the red in days with an attitude like that.

"You've already made quite a profit. That kid of yours drives a hard bargain."

"Like mother, like daughter," said Sam with a smile. "Condiments?"

He leaned across the round table and told her exactly what she could do with her condiments in a way that made her laugh. "You sure you never heard of me? Three appearances on *Night Line* with Koppel. Johnny Carson Show in 1986. A mention in *Time* and *Newsweek*—"

"I believe you, Murphy, I believe you!"

"*U.S. News* and *World Report*—"

"I admit your credits are impressive but I still don't know who you are." She patted his forearm much the same way she often patted her daughter's. "Don't be hurt. I've been so busy the last few years I only found out last week that Reagan's out of office."

"Sorry," O'Rourke said. "I'm having trouble adjusting to the civilian life. Unless you're a news junkie, there's no reason for you to know who I am."

"No apology needed."

"I sounded like a jerk."

"We all do sometimes."

"Turkey and tuna."

Sam blinked. "I beg your pardon?"

"The sandwiches. Turkey and tuna. Rye and whole wheat. Plenty of cole slaw and garlic dills, if you have them."

"You are one very strange man, O'Rourke." She grabbed the pen back from him and wrote down his order. "Pretzels? Peanuts?"

"We have a supplier."

They went over how many trays she would prepare, refrigeration requirements, delivery times.

"You know your stuff," he said, a note of admiration in his voice. "If you can cook, I've got it made."

"I'd better be able to cook," Sam said as she put the cap back on her pen and closed her notebook. "I intend to become rich doing it."

"Ambitious?"

Her jaw settled into its familiar granite line. "Extremely."

He leaned back in his chair, fingers tapping against the arm. "Your daughter's a lot like you."

"I know," Sam said, pride welling up inside her chest. "She believes she can have anything she wants, as long as she works for it." And, considering Patty's intellectual gifts, the sky was the limit.

"Do you believe the same thing?"

Sam thought about the rose-covered cottage and gingham apron she'd once believed would be hers, then contrasted it to the life she had now. "Yes," she said slowly. "I don't believe in setting limits on achievement." Truth to tell, she wouldn't trade the life she had now for any dream of the past.

His expression was warm and friendly and gently mocking. "Make a hell of a ham sandwich, do you, Samantha?"

"You better believe it!" Laughter, sudden and delighted, broke through her reserve. "The name's Sam, by the way."

He extended his hand. "Murphy."

They shook solemnly. Although she hated people who judged others by the force of a handshake, Sam couldn't help but note the assurance and strength in his grip.

"How would you feel about manning the grill a few nights a week until I hire a new chef?"

For a moment Sam was sorely tempted. "I love short-order cooking, but my schedule is packed between now and New Year's."

"Christmas shopping?"

Sam made a face. "Business. I'm opening my shop on New Year's Day."

He stared at her as if he'd seen a ghost. "No one opens a shop on New Year's Day. Everyone's home watching football and nursing champagne headaches."

"New Year's Day," she repeated, voice firm. "Think of how many football parties I can cater."

O'Rourke's grin faded. "What about your own party?"

"I don't have one."

"You go to a friend's house?"

Sam shook her head. "About the sandwiches," she said, looking to change the subject. "Maybe we should—"

"You have to go somewhere," O'Rourke persisted. "No one stays home on New Year's Eve."

"You must have been one heck of a reporter. It's none of your business, O'Rourke, but Patty spends the night at her grandparents' house and I usually work."

"I thought you were in cooking school or something."

"Catering firms go crazy during the holidays. I can pick up a month's wages with a few days' work and manage to keep the house warm in January as a result. Who am I to refuse?''

The twinkle in his hazel eyes was replaced by a laser beam of unashamed curiosity. "You hate Christmas."

"Don't be ridiculous!" *You're too good at this, O'Rourke. Go back to searching for Kremlin secrets.*

"It's written all over your face."

"That's fatigue."

"What about Patty? Kids live for Christmas."

"Patty does just fine at Christmas, don't worry."

"You decorate a tree?"

"Of course."

"You put up lights at the window?"

"Patty does."

"Do you send Christmas cards?"

"When I can afford the stamps."

The glitter in his eyes returned. "And you hate every minute of it."

"Damn right I do." Sam shoved her chair back and rose to her feet. "I'll drop off the sandwiches on my way to the train station tomorrow morning. Please have someone here to let me in. Seven-thirty, the latest." She turned to head for the door but he grabbed her wrist.

"Hit a nerve, didn't I?"

"I'm surprised you didn't recognize a closed door when you saw one."

"I didn't get to be a foreign correspondent by letting doors stay closed."

"Well, I have a news flash for you, O'Rourke— you're not a reporter anymore, you're a bartender in

New Jersey and how I feel about Christmas is none of your business.''

His own chair scraped against the floor as he stood up and faced her. His rugged features had lost the edge of humor and it occurred to Sam that she was alone in a bar with a group of men she knew next to nothing about.

''One question,'' he said, his voice gruff.

She swallowed hard. ''Just one then I'm out of here.''

''Does this mean you won't be making the sandwiches for us.''

''With what you're willing to pay me? You must be joking,'' said Sam. ''A deal's a deal.''

''You don't know how glad I am to hear you say that.'' O'Rourke broke into a crooked smile that was actually rather appealing, in an odd sort of way. ''I'm glad Patty brought us together.''

''So am I,'' said Sam. ''I think it be will profitable for both of us.''

''Yeah?'' said O'Rourke as he walked her to the door. ''I was thinking that it just might be fun.''

He didn't help her into her coat or walk her out to the parking lot or do any of the things a gentleman usually did. He was gruff, opinionated, self-centered and a lousy dresser but by the time Sam was halfway home she realized that Murphy O'Rourke was also one hundred percent right.

Fun!

Who'd have thought it?

Chapter Four

"Forget it," said Murphy when he turned around to face the gray inquisition after Sam said good-night. "She'll be cooking for us. Nothing more."

"She's a fine looking woman," said Joe, helping himself to another pint of draft. "Not all painted up like the one you brought around last Christmas."

"I like them all painted up," said Murphy, flipping the sign to Closed—and wondering when they'd take the hint.

"She looks to be a woman of fine breeding," Scotty pronounced.

"Don't go reading anything into it, Scotty. Strictly business."

"That was an exceptionally long business conversation, my boy. Certainly bar food does not require so intense a debate."

Murphy stifled a yawn. "We had a lot to talk about."

"Ham and cheese is that interesting?"

"Get off my back, will you, Scotty?" Murphy's tone was good-natured but exasperated. "We were talking about her kid."

"Acquiring a paternal instinct at this late date?"

Murphy grabbed a bar rag and swabbed down the counter by the sink. "Patty's a genius."

"All parents believe their offspring to be genius calibre."

"This kid's the real thing, Scotty. Certifiably brilliant."

"A child after my own heart." Scotty narrowed his eyes in thought. "What, may I ask, is she doing in a mediocre school like Harborfields?"

"You were at Princeton too long, MacTavish. Not everyone can afford snot-nosed prep schools for their kids."

"What does her father do for a living?" Scotty was of the old school and believed the male of the species should shoulder the greater portion of life's burdens.

The question brought Murphy up short. "I don't know," he said after a moment.

"Single mother?"

"Divorced, I guess," said Murphy, although they hadn't touched on anything quite that personal.

"You didn't see fit to ask?"

"It never came up."

"This child," said Scotty, following Murphy back to the office where he kept the bar receipt books. "What was it about her that put you in mind of me?"

Murphy sat on the edge of the metal desk. "Brainpower, Scotty. The kid has it in spades. Would you believe I spent five minutes with her and ended up hiring her mother to cook for the bar?"

Scotty's laugh filled the tiny office. "I'm seventy-two years old, my boy. I'd believe just about anything."

Murphy gave him the *Reader's Digest* version of the business negotiations played out that afternoon.

"A thirty percent markup at least," said Scotty.

"Try thirty-five."

"This child is a natural resource," Scotty declared. "No doubt she could alleviate the deficit in the blink of an eye."

"She did a hell of a good job alleviating her mother's deficit."

"Obviously Samantha is a marvelous cook."

"I hope so," Murphy mumbled.

"You hope so?" Scotty's eyes widened behind his glasses. "You haven't sampled her wares?"

"I tried some cookies."

"And...?"

"And nothing, Scotty. Christmas cookies. That's it."

"And you've hired this woman to handle the care and feeding of your valued customers?"

Murphy opened his mouth to speak but the retired professor was on a roll.

"This tavern provides more than libation for a thirsty traveler, Murphy. It's a haven for the lonely, a home for the homeless, a—"

"Give it a rest, will you, Scotty?" bellowed Murphy. "We're talking pizza and hamburgers here, not the salvation of the western world."

"The younger generation," said Scotty with a shake of his head. "You don't understand the value of a neighborhood pub."

Right again, Scotty. Murphy had spent his adult life running as far and fast from Rocky Hill as his ambition could carry him and the minute Bill O'Rourke was ready to take over again, Murphy would be on the next plane out.

FRANK GIFFORD was announcing the start of the fourth quarter of the football game when Patty heard her mother's Blazer chugging up the driveway. She leaped from the couch and peered out the window through a crack in the venetian blinds.

"Mom's home!"

"Is she smiling?" asked her Aunt Caroline, striking a carefree pose on the couch as if they both hadn't been waiting anxiously for Sam to hear all about her meeting with Murphy O'Rourke.

"I can't tell. She's up to her eyebrows in Shop-Rite bags."

"Your mother is a sick woman." Caroline stifled a yawn. "We sit up half the night waiting for her to return from an assignation with a foreign correspondent and she ends up pushing a cart at the supermarket. I'm ready to give up on her, Patricia."

The more Patty heard the name, the better she liked it. Why didn't it sound so wonderful when Mrs. Venturella called her Patricia? She pulled the drapes across the front window and curled up opposite Caroline. "She's whistling. That's a good sign."

"Knowing Sam, she might be whistling because she got a great deal on cauliflower."

Patty couldn't argue that statement; the past few years, her mother had been more interested in business than anything else on earth except for Patty herself. But this time was different; Patty was certain of it. How could her mom meet someone as perfect as Murphy O'Rourke and walk away unimpressed?

"Hi, Mom!" Patty trilled as Sam closed the front door behind her.

"Hello to both of you," said Sam as Patty jumped up to help her mother with the parcels. "I didn't know you'd still be here, Caroline."

Aunt Caroline had no time for small talk. "How long were you at the meeting?" she asked.

Patty's breath caught in her throat.

"Five minutes," said her mom.

"Five minutes!" Patty knew her voice sounded all high and squeaky like a little kid, but she couldn't help it. "You couldn't have spent just five minutes with him!" Murphy O'Rourke was exciting and smart and funny—everything that was just right for her mom. There was no way in the world they could have said everything that needed to be said in just three hundred seconds!

"Five minutes at the meeting," her mom repeated, her expression neutral.

Sam headed toward the kitchen with her parcels. Patty grabbed a bundle and followed after her mom, with Aunt Caroline close behind.

"C'mon, Mom," urged Patty as the grocery bag split and spilled the produce on the counter top. "Don't tease me like that."

"Patricia is right," said Caroline from the doorway. "She's too mature for such teasing."

"Patricia?" Patty's mom put two grocery bags down on the counter near the sink. "When did that happen?"

"Patricia is an elegant name, as befits this brilliant child," said Aunt Caroline in her loftiest manner.

Sam looked back at Patty. "What do you think about it?"

Patty shrugged, wishing the conversation would go back to what was really important: Murphy O'Rourke. "I like it. It makes me feel grown up."

Groaning, Sam unpacked two rolls of toilet paper and some hand soap from the first bag. "Make yourself useful, friend." She pressed the items into Caroline's arms. "Stash these in the back bathroom."

"Slave driver," muttered Caroline and disappeared down the dark hallway.

Sam turned back to her packages. Patty was almost beside herself with excitement, as if her skin had turned itself inside out and all of her nerve endings were dangling in the breeze.

"Do your homework?" Sam asked, her voice matter-of-fact.

"Hours ago."

"Did Caroline keep you from going to sleep?"

Patty shook her head. "I was staying up to see you." *Uh-oh.* From the way her mom's dark brows arched toward the ceiling, Patty knew she had made a strategic error. Time to retreat and regroup. She fiddled with a teaspoon resting alongside the stainless steel sink. "Did you meet Mr. O'Rourke?" she asked, as casually as she could manage.

Her mom nodded.

"Did you talk about the job?"

"All that money for so little work—it should be against the law!" Her mom shook her head in amazement. "You cooked up quite a deal for me, Patty."

Patty's spirits soared. "Did you…umm…did you like him?"

"He's not very good at business. I like that in a man."

"I think he's cute," said Patty, stepping out onto thin ice.

"Cute?" Her mom laughed out loud. "The man dresses like a bum."

Patty was highly insulted. Couldn't her mother see that Murphy O'Rourke was a free spirit? Free spirits didn't worry about three-piece suits and lace-up shoes. "I think he has style."

"Honey, that trench coat was the worst."

"It has character," Patty retorted. "Can you imagine, Mom, one time he left it on the Orient Express and they sent it back to him the very next day."

"No doubt," said her mother in that I-am-the-grownup tone of voice that Patty hated with all her heart. "The Orient Express has a reputation to consider."

Caroline came back into the kitchen, her coat slung over her arm. "Did I hear something about the Orient Express?"

Suddenly Patty didn't want to talk about Murphy O'Rourke any more. Her Aunt Caroline had a string of boyfriends, one ex-husband, and at least a dozen lovestruck suitors hoping for a chance to win her heart, and Patty would bet dollars to donuts that Caroline wasn't about to surrender her heart to any of them. She loved her godmother, but Caroline had a funny way of looking at men, almost as if they were windup toys and not real people.

Her mom didn't think like that, and Patty couldn't imagine Murphy O'Rourke being bossed around by anybody.

Patty raised up on tiptoe and peered into the grocery bag atop the microwave. "Three jars of dill pickles?" she asked, looking to change the subject.

Her mom grinned and removed a bread knife from the drawer near the sink. "Your Mr. O'Rourke requested them."

Was Patty just tired or were her mother's dark eyes sparkling with fun?

"Business, business, business," muttered Caroline, slipping into her coat. "I give up on you."

"Good," said Sam, slicing into a loaf of rye.

Good, thought Patty. This wasn't the time for Caroline to bring up the Christmas masquerade ball. Her mother could be real stubborn when she thought she was being tricked into doing something she didn't want to do. Grandpa Harry always said that Sam would rather be boiled in oil than be forced to change her mind.

"I'll pick you up at seven," Caroline said, hugging Patty then heading toward the back door.

"Seven!" Sam looked positively panicked. "Isn't that late?"

Caroline paused in the doorway. "Didn't I tell you? I'm driving in tomorrow morning. I have a stack of Carolina Herrera gowns to pick up from Old Frosty on East Sixty-third Street." Old Frosty was a society wife whose idea of fun was buying expensive designer dresses and never wearing them. Half of Aunt Caroline's stock was courtesy of Old Frosty. In fact, there were an awful lot of ladies like her who seemed to shop for a living. Patty couldn't understand it because there was nothing in the world she hated as much as being dragged into Macy's at Quakerbridge and forced to try on new clothes for her mom. Why anyone would think all that dressing and undressing was fun was beyond her.

Grownups could be very weird sometimes.

Her mom and Caroline talked for a few minutes, trying to arrange their schedule, then Caroline decided it wouldn't hurt to get a later start. She'd pick up Sam and her sandwiches, then ferry them over to O'Rourke's Bar and Grill at seven-thirty. "Old Frosty can wait," Caroline said with a laugh as she wound her scarf around her throat. "I want to get myself a look at Patty's dr—" Patty almost fainted, she was so scared. She faked a sneeze and sent a glass tumbling off the tabletop and crashing to the floor. Anything to keep Caroline quiet! Her aunt was about to say "dream man," she just knew it. If her mom got so much as the slightest hint of matchmaking—well, Patty couldn't bear to think about what would happen.

Patty jumped up to get the whisk broom and dustpan. What a close call that had been! She didn't take an easy breath until Aunt Caroline waved goodbye and hurried outside to her car.

"Don't you think you should go to sleep now, kiddo?" asked Sam after the car disappeared down the street. "It's after eleven."

She bet "Patricias" didn't have mothers who told them it was time for bed. "I want to see the Giant's win."

"Why is it I have the feeling you haven't paid one second's worth of attention to the game all night?"

Patty giggled—a very un-Patricialike thing to do— and snatched a piece of American cheese from the stack on the counter top. "Aunt Caroline doesn't like football. We talked mostly."

"And why is it I have the feeling that you talked mostly about me?"

Patty really tried to be honest all the time, and not telling her mother the one hundred percent truth made her feel kind of jumpy inside. She could just imagine what Sam would say if Patty told her that Caroline had bought tickets to the masquerade ball for both of them! The only thing that would make Sam angrier was knowing that Patty was envisioning Murphy O'Rourke as a permanent feature around their maple kitchen table.

"Maybe I am tired," she said. She didn't even have to fake a yawn. "I suppose I'll go to sleep now after all."

"Sounds like a good idea to me," said her mom with a knowing look. "You wouldn't want me to find out you'd been matchmaking now, would you?"

Patty felt like she did when she played dodgeball at school: her stomach tightened and it seemed as if all the air had been pulled out of her lungs.

"Are you mad?" To her horror, tears burned against her eyelids and she prayed she wouldn't do something as stupid and childish as crying.

"I should be," her mother said, leaning against the counter and taking Patty's trembling hands in her own cool ones, "but for some reason I'm not."

It's Murphy O'Rourke! thought Patty, her heart tumbling and twisting inside her chest. *How can you be mad at me when you've met the man of your dreams?*

"Murphy is a nice man," Sam continued, "and the deal you made is a good one."

"I knew it!" Patty crowed, her tears forgotten. "I knew you'd like him. I—"

The look on her mother's face made Patty's words die off abruptly.

"I'll enjoy my association with him this week but that's as far as it will go."

"But, Mom, I—"

"I won't fall in love with him, honey."

"How do you know?"

"He's not my type."

"He believes in artistic freedom."

"No castles in the air, Patty, please!" Sam pulled her into her arms and kissed the top of her head. Sometimes Patty thought her mother would still be kissing the top of her head when Patty was fifty years old and a Nobel Prize winner. "How on earth did I ever give birth to such an impossible romantic? Just because you're smitten with Murphy O'Rourke doesn't mean I should be."

"He's perfect, Mommy," she said, forgetting that she was way too old to call her mother by a baby name, "he really is. If you'd only—"

But her mother wasn't listening to any of it.

"You're enough, kiddo, you always have been. It's the two of us together, the way it should be."

"I hate him!" Patty exclaimed, surprising them both. "He ruined everything!"

"Now don't you go blaming Mr. O'Rourke because your plans went haywire, young lady. The poor man has no idea what you're up to and I intend to keep it that way."

"I don't mean Murphy," Patty said, starting to cry for real. "I mean *him*."

Patty could feel her mother tense up. "Ronald?"

"My *father*. If he hadn't been such a creep you wouldn't be stuck all alone with me today."

Patty felt like running away when she saw the tears glittering in her mother's eyes. "Don't go feeling sorry for me," Sam warned, her voice low and tender. "The best thing that ever happened to me was having you." She chucked Patty under the chin and Patty forced a smile despite herself. "The second best thing was not marrying your dad."

Patty didn't often feel like a dumb little kid. She understood more about science and math and physics than most grownups three times her age ever would. But it was times like this when she knew there was a whole scary world of things out there that she might never understand, no matter how colossal her I.Q. or how formidable her vocabulary.

"But I thought you loved him," she managed, trying to make all these puzzle pieces fit together the way they did on television. "Grandma Betty told me all those stories about the way you met. She showed me the pictures of you two at the junior prom."

"I did love him, honey, but there are times when love isn't enough to make things work out the way you want them to." Patty actually felt a sharp pain in the center of her chest as she watched her mother struggle for composure. "I—wasn't the kind of girl the Donovan's thought was right for their Ronald."

"Because you weren't from Princeton?"

"Because we weren't rich. Because we drove old cars and my father didn't dress up and wear a suit to work." Sam stopped and her eyes closed for one long moment. Then she looked into Patty's eyes. "Yes, we loved each other, but not enough to matter."

Patty was beyond hearing anything but the pain in her mother's voice. "I hate him," she said again, her voice shaky and thin with rage. "He shouldn't have listened. He should have come to your house one night and asked you to marry him and you both could have run away and been happy."

"Oh, my little girl." This time Patty didn't object to being called a little girl because that was exactly what she felt like. "I'm happy now, don't you know that? I have you and I have Grandma and Grandpa and Caroline and all of our friends and family and in a few weeks we'll have the store. I don't need anything else, honey. I have everything I could possibly want right here."

Oh, how much Patty wanted to believe her mother's words.

But deep in her heart Patty knew there was still an emptiness in her mother's heart same as there was in hers. An emptiness that only a husband and father could fill.

Murphy O'Rourke.

It just had to be.

Chapter Five

Patty woke up sick the next morning. The little girl was cranky and demanding, and nothing Sam could do was enough to soothe the child's ruffled feelings. As much as she wanted to stay home with her daughter, there was no way on earth she could miss her last day of school.

"Thank God for mothers," she said to Caroline when her friend showed up to drive them both into Manhattan. "I'm twenty-eight and I still need to be rescued from time to time." Betty would be there in half an hour to take over.

Caroline offered to wait for Sam to get free, but it quickly became apparent that the trays of sandwiches would never fit in the tiny sports car.

"Go," said Sam, waving her friend on. "No reason for both of us to be late." It was bad enough that she was running behind; the last thing she needed was to cause Caroline to miss her appointment with Old Frosty.

It was eight o'clock when she whipped into the parking lot of O'Rourke's Bar and Grill. Her heart was thudding at an alarming rate, and she took a few quick, deep breaths before unloading the sandwich trays and making her way to the locked front door. O'Rourke was bound to be furious and she didn't blame him. This certainly wasn't the best way to gain a reputation for a fledgling company.

"I can explain," she blurted the moment he opened the heavy front door and ushered her inside the dark and quiet bar.

"Patty's sick," he said, his voice husky as if he'd just climbed out of bed, which judging by the hour wasn't hard to believe. "Her fever is down to 100.5."

"She called you?"

"She called me." He took the trays from her and set them down on one of the scarred wooden tables near the front. "She said I shouldn't blame you for being late." His grin was sleepy and surprisingly appealing. "She told me you were only doing your maternal duty."

Sam groaned and wished she had a less verbally precocious child. "Believe it or not, I didn't put her up to it."

"I believe you. I haven't forgotten you have yourself one smart kid."

Sam's eyes suddenly widened as she realized he was barefoot, shirtless and wearing a pair of sweatpants with a blown-out right knee. "You'll be the one with the fever if you don't cover up. Hasn't anyone told you winter's almost here?"

"I don't feel the cold," he said matter-of-factly as he closed the door. "I just rolled out of bed and down the stairs to let you in."

"You live up there?"

"For the time being." He smothered a yawn with the back of his hand. "How about some coffee?"

"I don't dare. As it is, I'll be lucky if I make my train."

"Patty said you have your final exam today."

Sam arched a brow. "Patty seems to have told you quite a lot."

"Afraid so." He laughed and Sam found she liked the sound. "You're twenty-eight, unmarried, a budding entrepreneur, a great mother, a rotten house-cleaner, and an all-around swell person."

"I suppose you know my height, weight, and social security number, too." *We have to talk, Patty....*

He leaned against the bar and folded his arms across his broad chest. "About five-seven, maybe one hundred ten soaking weight."

"What about the social security number?"

"Give me five minutes on the telephone and I'll come up with it." He tilted his head a fraction. "So how close was I?"

"Five-seven and a quarter and too-close-for-comfort with the weight."

"You're too damned skinny as it is. You should gain a few pounds."

"I will," she said, casting a covert glance at her watch. "Wait until I open up the shop. Good food is one of my passions. I'll probably blimp up the first month."

"Big deal," he said, snapping his fingers. "If you're happy, what does it matter?"

"You're definitely a strange man, Mr.—"

"Murphy. I thought we settled that last night."

"Murphy. Most men judge a woman by the way she looks."

"Hey, don't get me wrong. I'm not saying you should turn into Roseanne Barr but ten pounds wouldn't hurt you."

"I'll keep that in mind."

"Besides, I didn't hire you to model clothes. I hired you to make sandwiches."

Laughter bubbled to her lips. "I think we should quit while we're ahead."

"I'm not known for my tact."

"Can't say I'm surprised." She adjusted her scarf and slipped on her gloves. "You do know what to do with all of this stuff, don't you?"

His brows slid together in an early-morning version of a scowl. Intimidating it wasn't. "What is there to do with sandwiches? You dump them on a plate and people help themselves."

"I wrote out all the instructions on a piece of stationery and taped it to the tray of ham and swiss."

"You're making me real nervous, Samantha."

"There's nothing to be nervous about." Men were terminally strange when it came to anything more complicated than a can opener and a microwave. "I made a few appetizers last night to practice for my final. Patty and I can't eat all of them so..." Her voice trailed off.

"Appetizers?"

"Nothing fancy. Just heat and eat. It's on the house."

"No way. What do I owe you?"

Sam thought about Patty and her killer business deal. "Believe me, you don't owe me a thing. You're paying me more than enough as it is."

He inclined his head in thanks and opened the door. "What about the trays?"

"I'll come back tonight after school to pick them up." A brisk wind whipped through the open door to the bar, and she saw gooseflesh form on his arms. "Put something on now, will you, please?"

He grinned and Sam found herself grinning back. She hadn't grinned in at least six or seven years.

"My male pulchritude too much for you, huh?"

"Definitely," said Sam as she turned to leave. "Especially this early in the morning."

"Later," said Murphy O'Rourke.

"Later," said Sam.

You're right about this one, Patty, she thought as she headed across the parking lot toward her Blazer. *A genuinely terrific man.* Murphy O'Rourke was funny and sharp and not all that bad looking without his shirt on. She liked his style and his bar and the way he treated women and children.

Too bad she wasn't interested.

MURPHY WATCHED SAM trot across the parking lot, her shapely rear end looking damn cute in those black pants. For a skinny woman, she had a surprising number of curves hidden beneath her loose clothing. Of course, he usually liked his women a bit on the *zaftig* side but Sam Dean wasn't half bad. There weren't many things Murphy liked before his first cup of coffee and to his amazement Sam had turned out to be easy on the nerves.

Who would've thought it?

He liked the way she seemed comfortable in her own skin, not looking for a way to be anyone other than exactly who she was. She seemed ambitious without being driven; sharp without being brittle; friendly without being pushy. She was the kind of woman you could kick back with and relax. Watch the game. Read the papers. Take to bed and—

No way. Some men liked long and lanky brunettes with small boobs and tight butts and eyes that glittered like onyx. Murphy would be the first to admit the combination had its charm, but he liked his women small, blonde and as big-breasted as possible. He also liked women who came unencumbered, and it wasn't hard to see Sam Dean came with quite a bit of baggage, including the delightful Patty. Although for some strange reason he couldn't imagine any man thinking of Patty Dean as an encumbrance.

He continued to watch as Sam climbed into her battered Blazer, revved up the engine, then zipped off down the road toward the Princeton Junction train station. He glanced up at the big round clock hanging near the door to the kitchen. In about nine hours she'd be back.

The thought made him smile.

"What's this?"

Murphy started in surprise and turned around to see his father, dressed and in an overcoat, poking the sandwiches on the top tray.

"Food," said Murphy. "Thanks to Earle and his sudden departure, we have a kitchen problem."

Bill O'Rourke grunted and peeled back the wrappings on a huge pile of perfectly sliced pickles. "Real fancy,'' he said with a sharp look at his son. "Who are you trying to impress?''

"Not you.'' He debated leaving it at that but his better instincts won out. "I hired a new caterer from Princeton Junction. She threw the appetizers in as an extra.''

"Free?''

"Is that so hard to believe?''

"Nothing's free in this world, boy. Thought you were old enough to realize that.''

Murphy was thirty-six years old. He'd traveled the world. He'd lived through a bad marriage and a worse divorce. He'd acquired a hide tough as shoe leather and a heart to match, but damned if his old man couldn't still find the right place to stick the knife.

"Sounds like you've been talking to Joey Boy again.''

"Your brother is worried about my future,'' Bill said.

"And I'm not?'' *Damn it. Don't let him bait you like this.*

"I didn't say that.''

"Yeah, but I suppose little brother did.''

"He thinks I should see a specialist in Florida.''

"Princeton doctors aren't good enough?''

"He thinks I should slow down.''

"Dr. Cohen thinks you aren't doing enough.''

"He thinks I should sell the bar.''

"And do what? Count your food stamps?''

His father's cheeks reddened. "Joey thinks I should retire. He thinks I should sell the bar and the house and—''

"Yeah, don't tell me. Move down to Florida and turn into a sunburned old man with nothing but time on his hands." Murphy waved his arms in disgust. "I've heard it all before."

"At least I'd have family down there."

Good going, Dad. Now you're bringing out the heavy artillery. "Carole and Jay and the kids don't count?" *Fooled you, didn't I, Dad. You thought I was going to count myself in, too.*

"Of course they count," said Bill, sounding uncertain. "But *you* aren't going to be here forever."

"That's right," said Murphy, struggling to remember that his old man was still under a doctor's care, "and you're not going to be recuperating forever. Things will get back to normal soon enough."

He's scared. He's had a heart attack. Remember everything Dr. Cohen told you about cardiac patients. Don't blow up!

Bill folded the plastic wrap back over the appetizers, his fingers trembling with the effort. It was almost enough to make Murphy relent.

Almost, but not quite.

"Stein called last night," Bill said, meeting Murphy's eyes. "He says he wants you back on the paper."

"He says a lot of things," Murphy mumbled, "some of which are even true."

"He says he'll give you a raise."

"I'll tell him where he can stick his raise."

"He said you can have the city beat. The tri-state gubernatorial coverage. A Sunday spot on *Face the City*. Anything."

"Right. Anything but freedom of speech." Murphy stormed over to the coffeepot and poured himself a steaming cup. "Forget it."

Bill fumbled through his pockets and extracted a stick of gum that he unwrapped and folded into his mouth. "You come rolling in here, playing savior, and think you can make everything right, when you haven't bothered to come around in years."

Murphy threw his hands in the air. "Isn't it too early in the morning for venom, Pop?" It wasn't like he'd abandoned his father then come around looking for an inheritance.

"You wanted out from the minute you were born."

"Can you blame me? This wasn't exactly a happy home we had here."

"I'm not made of money," Bill said. "You can't live here forever."

Murphy, who had not only been paying his way but everybody's else's, looked up from his cup at the man who'd fathered him but never understood one damned thing about who and what he was. "You've said that before," he said quietly. "On my eighteenth birthday."

Both men fell silent. Murphy had walked out that day within half an hour of Bill's terse pronouncement. He swore Rocky Hill was history and so was his father; the only way he'd come back was in a chauffeur-driven limousine with money to burn. It had taken eight years of struggling but on his twenty-sixth birthday he'd pulled up to O'Rourke's Bar and Grill in a monster Caddy limo with a full bar in the back and treated his father and his brother to a day at the track. On him. All of it. Murphy was a fountain of money that day and not even the fact that it took him six months to pay off the bills was enough to sour the sweet taste of victory.

For one fleeting moment, he'd been someone in his father's eyes and in his brother's. There'd never been another moment like it.

He looked at his father. *And probably never would be.*

"Want some coffee?" he asked, reaching for a clean cup.

"I'm on my way out," said Bill, buttoning up his coat.

"Need a lift?"

Bill shook his head. "Tessie Gargan is picking me up on the corner."

"Going any place special?"

"Doc Cohen wants me in."

"Good luck," said Murphy. "Maybe you'll be kicking me out of here sooner than you think."

Bill paused in the doorway, his fair Irish skin flooded with color again. "Nobody's forcing you to stay, boy. You can go back to your fancy friends anytime you want."

"Yeah, Pop," said Murphy when the door slammed shut behind his father. "You're welcome."

But then he had no right to expect thanks. His father needed help. His sister couldn't provide it. His brother had bailed out to Florida and a ritzy law practice. Only Murphy remained; volatile, greedy, *unemployed* Murphy. And it was Murphy who came back to the place he'd struggled to escape from for so many years, only to discover that the more things change, the more they stay the same.

All his life, Bill O'Rourke had avoided emotions—
both his own and those of his two combative sons. His
heart attack back in October had changed many things
but not that one basic part of Bill's personality and
Murphy doubted if anything ever would.

CAROLINE COULD BE BOSSY, annoying and generally
a pain in the neck, but she was one terrific best friend.

Who else would sit at the corner of West Fiftieth
and Eighth Avenue in the pricey sports car piled high
with designer gowns just so she could drive New
York's newest cooking school graduate back home to
New Jersey that afternoon?

"I owe you one," Sam said as she settled into the
cushioned leather seat and rested her head back.

Caroline chuckled and switched on the stereo sys-
tem. "Just you remember that when the time comes."

Soft, lush music filled the small car as the Jaguar
inched its way toward the Lincoln Tunnel. Sam closed
her eyes and let herself drift lazily along on a cloud of
her friend's ubiquitous Chanel No. 5. Neatly stacked
on the tiny back seat, padded with tons of tissue to
prevent wrinkles, were three glorious Cinderella ball
gowns, the latest acquisitions from Old Frosty. A pale
tea rose with delicate seed pearls tracing the curves of
the bodice. A red beaded gown made for grand en-
trances. And a magnificent, fairy tale of a satin dress
in a sapphire blue so deep and luminous that the sight
of it had made Sam almost weep with joy.

A sigh threatened to escape, and she quickly translated it into a yawn. All Caroline needed was to know
how badly Sam would love to primp and fuss and
dress to the nines and dazzle the denizens of Prince-

ton at the masquerade ball; there would be no living
with the pressure her best friend would put on her.
Anyone—even Sam—could spare just one Saturday
night to live a dream but the rock bottom truth of the
matter was the hundred-dollar ticket fee might as
well be ten thousand. Money—wouldn't you just
know that would be the problem.

But, oh, how wonderful it was to daydream about
it! Sam wasn't given to flights of fancy the way Patty
was, but it seemed as if the ball gowns whispered
stories with each rustle of satin and silk. Dazzling
women and handsome men in all their splendor,
waltzing on a shimmering marble dance floor to the
strains of Strauss. Exciting flirtations behind the de
rigeur white velvet masques. Caroline would look like
a movie star in the Schiaparelli gown while Sam—

Sam would what?

She closed her eyes more tightly and concentrated.
It wasn't as if she had no imagination, after all. She
was a world-class daydreamer, but try as she might
Sam couldn't conjure up one single vision of herself in
anything but baggy cords and a black sweater.

She could come up with an elegant upswept hairdo
only to pan down to her trusty Reeboks and sweat
socks. Or she dreamed up a pair of pricey Maud Fri-
zon pumps with bejeweled buckles and teamed them
with her ragged jeans. But even more horrifying was
the image of herself all decked out in Old Frosty's
finery but with a face devoid of makeup and her ov-
ergrown hair pulled back in a ponytail.

It was as futile an undertaking in her daydreams as
it was in real life. She was plain Sam Dean, nothing

more, who had a daughter to provide for and a future to plan.

PATTY'S GRANDMA, Betty Dean, glanced at the thermometer and smiled. "Down another half degree, Patty. I think you'll live."

"Can I have some more ice cream?"

"You had some at lunchtime."

"Please, Grandma. My throat's sore and the ice cream makes it feel better."

Grandma Betty pursed her lips but Patty saw the twinkle in her bright blue eyes. "Maybe."

Grandma bustled out of Patty's bedroom, leaving behind the smell of cinnamon and brown sugar, and Patty had little doubt a bowl of vanilla ice cream wouldn't be long in coming. Smiling, she nestled back under her covers and thumbed through the newest issue of *Time Magazine*. Not even a discussion of supply-side economics could pique her interest. She glanced at her watch. Back at school they were just starting math class, and Patty had been looking forward to a special project Mr. Berman had promised would keep her busy for a while.

Except for the vanilla ice cream, Patty hated being sick because being sick meant staying home from school. Oh, she wouldn't admit it even to her best friend, Susan, but she looked forward to school each morning the way other kids looked forward to summer vacation. She loved the feeling of excitement when she sat down in class and opened her book, even if that excitement wasn't quite as much fun as it used to be. It seemed the longer she was in school, the harder the teachers at Harborfields Elementary found it to keep ahead of her.

Lately, Patty had been spending a lot of time in the Rocky Hill library, checking out big fat books on physics and calculus and advanced methods of food production for the Third World. The librarian said that pretty soon Patty would have to go to the big Somerset County library in Bridgewater. "Can't keep up with you, honey," the woman had said with a shake of her gray head. "Don't know if the whole state can for long."

Now and then she'd hear teachers whisper about special classes and what a shame it was a child so bright was languishing in a school like theirs, and a cold knot of fear would form in Patty's stomach and made her wish she could be like everybody else. She loved her friends and she loved her teachers, and she couldn't imagine going to school any place but Harborfields. Sometimes she would see her mother's face grow all cloudy and sad looking when she thought Patty wasn't looking, and Patty found herself scared and confused and angry that her mom had to work so hard for things other people took for granted.

If she had a father, it all would be different. She just knew it. When there was a father in the house, everything was better. Oh, she knew real families weren't like the old TV shows where father always *did* know best and mothers like Donna Stone and Margaret Anderson spent their afternoons planning their evening dinner menus. Real families weren't even like the Huxtables or the Seavers where both mom and dad went to work and the kids had keys to the house. Real families didn't always fit together the way they should;

real families didn't always like each other; but real families stayed together forever and that was the one thing Patty wanted.

She loved going to Susan's and listening to Mrs. Gerard complain about Mr. Gerard's magazines scattered around the family room and the toothpaste tube left uncapped in the bathroom. Even though Patty was only ten years old and had never had a father of her own, she somehow knew that Mrs. Gerard's griping was a form of affection and she wished with all her heart she had a father around the house to scatter magazines around and leave toothpaste tubes uncapped and make her mother smile.

Murphy O'Rourke could make her mother smile.

The magazine slipped from her fingers and she closed her eyes. Grandma Betty was whistling in the kitchen and Patty could hear the low mumble of the television set tuned to *As the World Turns*. She didn't want to fall asleep. Any minute Grandma would be bringing in a dish of vanilla ice cream, but it was so cozy there tucked under the covers. From somewhere came the sound of a doorbell ringing and Patty wondered who would come calling in the middle of a regular day...

"Honey, I'm home!" Murphy O'Rourke, looking tall and handsome in his corduroy jacket and worn raincoat, stepped through the front door of their house in Rocky Hill.

"Darling!" Sam O'Rourke swept into the room, her full skirts billowing around her knees. "Dinner is almost ready. I made your favorite—chili and spare ribs." Sam's dark hair was swept off her face and fell below her shoulders in glossy ringlets. Her makeup

*was perfect. Her frilly white apron looked fetching
against her pale blue dress.*

*Murphy tossed down his briefcase on the piano
bench and pulled her into his arms. "Just think," he
said, "if it hadn't been for Patty, we never would have
met."*

*"Yes," said Sam with a delighted sigh. "We owe this
all to our daughter. Patricia Dean O'Rourke, the
youngest graduate in M.I.T.'s history...."*

"No man is luckier," said Murphy.

"No woman is happier," sighed Sam.

And no dream had ever been better.

Chapter Six

"Five minutes," said Sam as Caroline turned off the engine and let out the clutch later that evening. "I'll pick up the empty trays, get a bit of feedback from O'Rourke, and we're on our way."

"Don't rush on my account," said Caroline, reaching for the door handle.

"You don't have to come with me." Sam swung her legs out of the low-slung car. "I'll be back before you know it." The very last thing she needed was Caroline's opinion of Murphy O'Rourke.

Sam crunched across the gravel driveway with Caroline's footsteps crunching right behind. Boisterous male laughter seeped through the walls of O'Rourke's Bar and Grill, along with the friendly blare of big-band music popular around the time of the Second World War.

"They sound like a happy group of campers," Caroline observed as they paused in front of the door.

Sam resisted the urge to smooth her bangs and refresh her lipstick. Mustering up a smile, she opened the door and ushered Caroline inside.

Her friend looked at the crowd and went pale. "Samantha, these men are seventy, if they're a day."

"I know."

Caroline's shock was almost comical. "How old *is* O'Rourke, anyway?"

Sam was about to answer when she heard footsteps behind her, then a male voice.

"Hi, Sam."

Both women turned as Murphy O'Rourke, clad in a putty-colored shirt and a pair of baggy cords, strolled up to them. He carried a bottle of Schnapps in one hand and a bar towel in the other.

"Caroline," said Sam with a wide grin, "this is Murphy."

He tucked the bar towel in his belt and extended his hand. "You're the one with the clothes shop."

Caroline shook his hand and shot Sam another quelling glance. "You've been talking about me?"

"Patty has," said Murphy. "She called to tell me you both would be stopping by."

Sam's face flashed with embarrassment. God only knew what else her voluble daughter might have told O'Rourke. "You might want to consider an unlisted number. Patty seems to have taken quite a liking to you."

He shrugged amiably. "It's mutual. She's some piece of work."

Sam warmed at his words. "That she is. She's always trying to set me up wi—" *Oh, no, Dean. Keep your foot out of your mouth for a change.* She gestured toward the busy saloon. "You're busy. Why don't you show me where the trays are and we'll be on our way."

O'Rourke's hazel eyes were friendly and disarmingly direct. "You in a rush?"

"We're going out to dinner."

"I hope you don't have reservations."

She blinked. "I beg your pardon?"

He inclined his head toward Caroline who—amazingly—was now perched atop Scotty's table and laughing uproariously with his companions. "I don't think she's in any hurry."

"So I see." Sam glanced again at her best friend. "It would serve her right if I took her Jag and aimed it for the Pizza Hut."

"Patty said it's a celebration." He led her toward the bar where she claimed a stool on the end. "Congratulations. What are you celebrating?"

"My last day of school. If I never see Manhattan again it'll be too soon. I hate that city."

His expression darkened, and she remembered that Manhattan had been his stomping grounds before he walked off the job at the *Telegram*.

"Sorry, Murphy. I have strong feelings about New York City and most of them aren't nice."

"New York's a great place if you're rich enough to enjoy it. Fortunately I was rich enough." He reached under the bar and pulled up a bottle of asti spumante. "How about a toast to your graduation?"

She hesitated a moment. "I haven't eaten yet today. I might end up with a lampshade on my head."

He grinned. "I'd offer you some food but they cleaned me out."

Her eyes widened. "They ate everything? Even those bacon-and-mushroom pinwheels?"

"Even the pinwheels. I'd thought this meat-and-potatoes bunch would turn their noses up at fancy stuff like that."

She ran her hand along the brass rail, admiring the old-fashioned workmanship that had gone into the bar itself. "The world's full of surprises."

"Like that kid of yours," he said, popping the cork on the asti spumante.

"Like that kid of mine." She cast another glance at Caroline who paid her not the slightest heed. "Genius doesn't exactly run in my family."

He reached over and pulled down two flute glasses from the rack. "What about her father's family?"

"If genius ran in their family, maybe they'd be smart enough to appreciate their granddaughter."

"Their loss. I can't imagine anybody meeting Patty and not liking her."

Of course it was much more complicated than that and they both knew it. Not the sort of thing you discussed with a man you barely knew.

She watched as he poured the Italian champagne into the glasses. Murphy O'Rourke had nice hands, large and well formed, with a dusting of sandy-colored hair. His nails were cared for but not manicured. Sam hated men who wore clear polish and had their hair permed every few weeks. From the looks of O'Rourke's mop, he rarely paid a visit to the barber, which was all right by Sam.

He handed her a flute of asti spumante, then raised his glass. "To your success."

She raised her own in answer. "To a wonderful future for all of us."

They touched glasses. Sam sighed in pleasure as the bubbly golden liquid slithered down her throat. Normally talk of Patty's father or grandparents was enough to send Sam into a black cloud of depression, equaled only by her own reluctance to admit someone as dear as her little girl could mean so little to her own flesh and blood.

There was something about O'Rourke that rattled her defenses and loosened her tongue. He was as straightforward as a mug of draft. He had told her he wasn't known for his tact, and his behavior had borne out that statement, but somehow Sam found his blunt talk refreshing, instead of abrasive.

"I should get going." Sam polished off the rest of the Italian champagne and thanked God she wasn't driving for her head was buzzing rather nicely at that moment. "I have to be home by eleven."

Murphy chuckled and shot her a curious look. "A curfew at your age?"

She made a face at him. "My dad's babysitting Patty. Eleven's *his* bedtime."

He looked down at the battered Seiko on his wrist. "You're running out of time."

"Don't I know it." Across the room, Caroline was bent over the checker board with the apparent concentration of a nuclear physicist on the verge of a big discovery. "I'm ready to eat your bar stools." She cast him a mournful look. "Do you have any pretzels?"

O'Rourke's hazel eyes twinkled with a wicked light. "You can do better than that."

"I can?"

He reached for Sam's hand and drew her to her feet. "Let's go."

"THEY'RE GOING to be furious," said Sam, ten minutes later as they took their seats at Tony's Pizzeria.

"No, they're not," said Murphy.

"We shouldn't have done this."

"Of course we should have."

"What about the bar?"

"Scotty will keep things running."

"Caroline will kill me."

"Do you care?"

A laugh escaped Sam. "Not at the moment." She sighed with pleasure. "You were right, Murphy. This pizza is fantastic!"

"Worth the walk?"

"Even in a blizzard!" Sam had grumbled as they walked the two blocks to Tony's in a bitter wind, but she had to admit it was worth it. "The question is—how do we get the rest of the pizzas back to the bar before they turn into popsicles?"

Murphy gestured toward a sign near the cash register. "Tony delivers."

She stopped, pizza halfway to her mouth. "You could have called in the order."

"Sure I could have." He sprinkled crushed red pepper on his slice. "But you have to admit it's quieter here."

It was also more private. There had been thirty pairs of eyes trained intently upon them back at O'Rourke's. Thirty pairs of ears straining to hear every word that passed between them. Not that their words were particularly interesting or intimate, but such avid attention had made Sam a bit uncomfortable, especially with Caroline's bright blue eyes following Sam's every move.

Murphy might be a well-known figure at Tony's, but Sam wasn't and she found herself delighting in her anonymity. She could eat and drink and laugh all she wanted and not one single member of her family was around to wonder what was *really* going on. Sure, Caroline would have a few questions but Sam was certain she could handle her friend's curiosity.

Her own curiosity, however, was something else again as she pretended to concentrate her attention on her pizza. Truth was, it was Murphy O'Rourke who had her wondering.

"Hot peppers?" asked Murphy, pushing the container toward her.

"No, thanks."

"Cheese?"

"Not right now."

That wonderful lopsided grin tilted his mouth. "Questions?"

She leaned across the table. "What are we doing here?"

"You don't like it?"

"I love it."

"Great. I thought you would."

"You should be back at the bar."

"I needed a break. I was ODing on cigar smoke."

She nodded and sat back in her chair, chewing thoughtfully. *So, what did you expect, Dean? A declaration of love?* He wanted to get out and stretch his legs and grab a bite to eat. There was no mystery in that, no hidden romance. She refused to acknowledge a twinge of disappointment and instead grabbed for the hot peppers and sprinkled them liberally on her second slice of pizza.

Tony was whistling behind the counter as he packed the six pies into their boxes. The savory smells of onion and pepperoni and sausage filled the air.

"Do you always treat your customers this well?" Sam asked after Tony's delivery boy staggered out to the truck, unable to see over the stack of boxes.

"Good customer relations," he said with a shrug. "Keeps 'em coming back for more."

"You're a nice guy, O'Rourke. Why don't you just admit it?"

"Nice guys don't make good foreign correspondents. Looks lousy on the resume."

She thought about a third slice of pizza, hesitated, then reached for it, anyway. "I thought you were a city beat reporter."

"That was my last gig. Before that I spent ten years in Europe."

No wonder his trench coat had looked so battered; it had served as the official costume of the peripatetic correspondent. Why that should make her feel sad was beyond Sam. "Footloose and fancy-free, I suppose."

"Footloose and fancy-free except for a three-year marriage."

"Kids?"

"Nope."

"Your wife didn't like to travel?"

"My wife loved to travel," O'Rourke said, "but she didn't like traveling with me."

Sam took a bite of pizza, cheese stretching out like a white rubber band, and studied him intently as she chewed. "Are you over her?"

"Completely." His look matched hers in intensity. "How about you—divorced?"

"Never married."

"Does he see Patty?"

"About as often as Mr. Spock has sex—every seven years or so."

Murphy's use of language was salty and right on target.

"I've called him that a time or two myself," said Sam.

"He's missing out on a great kid."

"Serves him right," said Sam, her tone angry. "Unfortunately Patty's missing out on having a father."

"Does she miss him?"

"It's not Ronald Donovan she misses. It's having a real, live, seven-days-a-week father."

He leaned forward, eyes focused squarely on her. It wasn't hard to see how effective a reporter he must have been; there was something vaguely intimidating in his body language and intensity that could force state secrets out of shadowy hiding places. "How do you feel about that?"

She shrugged, wishing they'd stayed back in the crowded, noisy bar where a conversation like this could never have gotten off the ground. "Patty's a born romantic, Murphy. She believes in love at first sight, happily ever after and Donna Reed."

His intensity softened, and she thought she saw something akin to understanding in his eyes. "Nothing so terrible about that, is there, Sam?"

"Only if you're ten years old and you really think it can happen."

"It happens sometimes."

"Maybe," said Sam, "but not to anyone I know."

He started to say something then stopped on the first syllable.

"Go ahead," said Sam. "Tell me I'm a cynic. You won't be the first."

"That's not what I was going to say."

"Don't tell me you agree with Patty."

"I'm too cynical, myself, for that." He looked over at Sam and an uneasy feeling built inside her stomach. "I almost wonder if Patty—" He stopped, shaking his head. "No. That's too ridiculous."

"What is?" How she managed to sound cool and collected was beyond Sam.

"Do you think she was trying to set us up?"

Sam started to choke on her pizza and she had to grab quickly for her beer before O'Rourke vaulted the table and began administering the Heimlich Maneuver.

"Stupid idea, right?" asked O'Rourke once she caught her breath.

"Stupid idea," she managed. *You're too good at this, O'Rourke. You should be back pounding the political beat.* Her little red-haired daughter was a born matchmaker. No one from the butcher at Shop-Rite to her pediatrician had escaped Patty's scrutiny. Sam liked to tease her, saying she had a Noah's Ark mentality but Patty truly believed in a couples—only world and had made it her business to see that Sam found her better half.

That Murphy could figure that out after only one meeting was frightening.

"So you're not looking for a husband?"

Sam shook her head. "Afraid not. I've been waiting so long to open my store that nothing short of an earthquake could tear me away from it."

"I still don't know exactly what kind of store you're opening. Is it a deli?"

Now this was territory she was familiar with. "Delis are for Rocky Hill, O'Rourke. I'm talking pure Princeton cuisine."

"I thought you were a takeout service."

Sam lifted her chin in a parody of the proper Princeton matron. "Upscale takeout service, thank you very much. Not a pastrami on rye to be found."

He made a face. "Not another pasta palace I hope."

"Pasta salads are trendy, O'Rourke. I thought you ersatz New Yorkers know all about being trendy."

"All I know is that spaghetti belongs on a plate with meatballs. Case closed."

Sam couldn't help laughing out loud. "You sound like my father. He thinks the only good chicken dinner comes straight from the Colonel's bucket."

O'Rourke grinned but maintained his position. "I think I'd like your father." He placed another slice of pizza on her plate then helped himself as well. "So how did you end up in the world of sushi and potato skins?"

"I'm a domestic creature. I grew up mixing brownies and making meat loaf suppers. It's the only marketable skill I have. Unfortunately you can't make a living slinging corned beef hash and chicken fricassee around here."

"So you're going where the market is."

"Exactly." She told him the location of her store and watched with satisfaction as his eyes widened with respect.

"I'm impressed," he said.

"So am I," said Sam. "I never thought I'd find a place so close to the railroad station."

"Hungry executives will fall out of the train and into your shop."

"That's the general idea."

His expression was comically sorrowful. "Now if you were cooking real food, I'd say you had a winner there."

Sam, whose own tastes ran more toward meat loaf than blackened red fish, shook her head. "Sorry, O'Rourke. Marketing 101—I intend to supply exactly what they demand."

"I think you're going to make a fortune."

"I hope so. Patty's the most important thing in my life. She deserves the best I can possibly provide."

He nodded as if he really understood. "I'm angling for another overseas spot with UPI. The minute my father's back behind the bar, I'm out of here."

"It looks like we both have our heads on straight, doesn't it?" asked Sam.

"We know what we want and how to go about getting it. Can't ask for more out of life than that."

"No," said Sam after a moment, thinking about the delights to be found in a warm restaurant on a cold winter's night with a man who could actually become a friend. "I don't suppose you can."

THE WALK BACK to O'Rourke's felt wonderful to Sam, sated as she was after the pizza feast at Tony's.

The wind was fierce, and they walked quickly, with their heads down. They didn't talk, but then, they didn't need to. She felt as comfortable with Murphy as if she had known him forever.

Pizza seemed to have worked wonders with the crowd at the bar. Sam had expected a barrage of questions—especially from Caroline—but their return to O'Rourke's was greeted with nothing more than a chorus of praise for the pizzas.

She sat down at the bar and watched as Murphy got to work. O'Rourke's Bar and Grill did a brisk, steady business. Customers arrived and departed with the predictability of a train schedule and there was no one who didn't have a good word for Murphy. He really had grown up in the tavern, Sam thought, as she watched an elderly woman with sleek silver hair and a quick laugh chuck Murphy under his chin.

Many of these customers had known Murphy since he was a little boy, and Sam found their affection for the former foreign correspondent endearing. Not that the elder O'Rourke was forgotten, however; you had only to listen to some of the stories told by the tavern regulars to understand just how sorely he was missed. Bill O'Rourke had opened the doors in the late forties and those doors had remained open ever since. There seemed to be some talk among the regulars about Bill being afraid of getting back to the daily grind after his heart attack, but Murphy never entered into these conversations. He just smiled and poured another draft and said, "Isn't it great about those Giants?"

Sam wasn't inclined toward on-the-spot analysis. As a rule, she was too busy to spend much time digging into psyches—her own or anybody else's. But there was something about Murphy O'Rourke that made her wish she'd be around long enough to figure out what made him tick. She'd never known an honest-to-goodness man of the world before. Why, he'd been to places she'd never dreamed of going. Bangkok. Peru. The deserts of Saudi Arabia. Sam had been content to remain in the town where she was born, in the neighborhood where she'd grown up, surrounded by people who knew her as well as she knew her own daughter.

It wasn't hard to imagine O'Rourke tossing down his bar apron and grabbing his trench coat the moment his dad stepped back into the picture.

No, she thought, watching as he fixed an Irish Coffee for Scotty, no matter how hard Patty wished for it, she'd picked the wrong man this time around. Murphy O'Rourke wasn't going to be around for the long haul. He probably had his suitcases packed and at the ready so he could be on the next plane out the minute his father was ready to take over the bar again.

The rest of the evening sped by in a blur of laughter and song. Caroline took over the upright piano in the back of the bar room and before too long the old timers were raising their voices to tunes Sam remembered from vintage World War II movies: "Don't Sit Under the Apple Tree," "Rum and Coca Cola." She closed her eyes and imagined she was at a U.S.O. dance, jitterbugging with a fresh-faced sailor who was on his way to battle....

"You're not singing."

She opened her eyes in time to see Murphy slide a mug of hot coffee across the bar to her.

"Thank your lucky stars," she said, holding back a yawn. "I could clear your bar in a matter of seconds."

"Maybe you should give me a few choruses of something loud and off-key. It's almost midnight. It's time some of these—"

"Midnight!" Sam leaped to her feet. "I have to go!"

"What happens now? Do you turn into a pumpkin?"

"No, but Caroline's Jag might."

"Can you fit those trays into a sports car?"

"Caroline said we'll tie them to the bumper if we have to." She extended her hand. "I've had a terrific evening."

"Sorry you missed out on the Pizza Hut?"

"Not a bit. You were right about Tony's—definitely the best place in town."

He shrugged in that offhanded way she was coming to know. "I couldn't let you starve, could I? There'd be no one to make the sandwiches for tomorrow."

"A practical man, Murphy O'Rourke." And a nice one. A cushy assignment like this would go a long way toward pushing Fast Foods for the Fast Lane into the black.

She hoped he took his time finding himself a cook.

THE BAR CLEARED OUT soon after Sam and her friend left. All except for Scotty.

"Need a ride?" Murphy asked, wiping down the bar and dumping ice down the sink. "I'll run you home if you want."

"I have my car," said Scotty.

Murphy eyeballed the coffeepot. "I think there's enough for another cup."

"Caffeine after midnight is my arch enemy, Murphy."

Murphy poured himself a cup and leaned against the bar. "Okay, friend, out with it. What's on your mind?"

"You're perceptive, my boy."

"Not particularly," said Murphy. "You're an open book."

"Has it occurred to you that the Masquerade Ball is this Saturday?"

"Big deal." The last thing on Murphy's mind was getting all decked out in a tux and plastering a velvet mask on his kisser.

"Caroline plans to attend."

"I hope she has a great time." He took a sip of coffee and battled down the urge to pour sugar into the deadly brew. He wondered if Sam was going to the ball and had the feeling Scotty had the answer, but he refused to give the professor the satisfaction. "Did she promise you a dance?"

Scotty sat up straighter, his tweeds fairly bristling with self-satisfaction. "The last waltz."

Murphy gave the man a friendly punch in the shoulder. "You old dog. Nice going. Next thing I know you'll be asking her to go as your date."

"That thought had occurred to me," Scotty said, "but unfortunately she is already spoken for." Scotty was receiving a special Princeton citizenship award and Murphy knew the dapper professor would have loved to show up with a beautiful blonde on his well-tailored arm.

"Too bad," said Murphy.

"Quite," said Scotty.

"You could take Angela."

Scotty flashed him a lethal look. Waitress Angela Fennelli and Edmund "Scotty" MacTavish were the proverbial oil and water. "To be truthful, I already have another prospect in mind."

Murphy threw his head back and laughed out loud. "You've been holding out on me." He straddled a chair across from Scotty. "Who's the lucky woman?"

"You are, Murphy my boy. You're going to be my date."

CAROLINE WAS STRANGELY QUIET on the way home and Sam would have been suspicious if it wasn't for the fact her friend had already said yes, she'd be happy to stop at the all-night Shop-Rite so Sam could pick up a few extra fixings for the tomorrow's sandwich trays and no, it wasn't a bother.

Caroline pulled her sports car right up to the front and waited while Sam ran in and grabbed a few cans and jars of goodies she knew Scotty and Joe and the others would enjoy. Hadn't Murphy said he was crazy about olives? She grabbed a can on her way to the checkout and chalked it up to customer relations.

"Thanks," said Sam as she folded herself back into the low-slung car. "I hope I didn't take too long."

"Not at all," said Caroline as she drove out of the parking lot. In profile she appeared to be smiling. "I hope you got everything you need."

Sam swiveled around in her seat and took a close look at her best friend. Bad enough she'd be going home to an irate father. The last thing she needed was a mysterious friend. "Okay, out with it. Let's get it out of the way."

Caroline batted her eyelashes the way she had at Scotty. "Whatever are you talking about?"

"Murphy."

"A lovely man," said Caroline, her tone bland. "He makes wonderful coffee."

"That's not what I mean."

Caroline glanced quickly in the rearview mirror. "Then perhaps you should be more explicit."

"The matchmaking," said Sam. "When is it going to start?"

"I'm not going to matchmake."

Puzzled, Sam leaned back in her seat. "Don't tell me you didn't like Murphy." Caroline and Patty were two-of-a-kind when it came to finding possible husbands for Sam.

"He was quite pleasant."

"But—?"

Caroline shrugged her elegant shoulders. "But I can see he plainly isn't your type."

"Why don't you think he's my type?"

"I would think that's obvious."

"Because he's a bartender?" Although Caroline was a product of Rocky Hill same as Sam, she tended to be class conscious.

"I thought he was a foreign correspondent."

"Yes."

"And a reporter for the *Telegram*?"

"Yes, he was that, too," said Sam, "but he's between jobs."

"Oh. So he's unemployed."

"He's not unemployed." *Shut up, Sam! You sound like you're defending the man.* "He's helping out with the family business."

"He's not for you."

"You're talking to the daughter of a plumber, Caroline. There's nothing wrong with running a bar."

"And you're talking to the daughter of a mechanic. You're not telling me anything I don't know."

"So what's the problem? Why aren't you pushing Murphy and me together?"

"Chemistry." Caroline cast her a quick glance but Sam couldn't read her expression in the dark car. "There isn't any."

"I resent that."

"Sorry, but it's true. He's just not interested in you."

Sam's jaw settled into that old stubborn line. "You mean, *I'm* not interested in *him*."

"You heard exactly what I said, Sam. He's not interested in you sexually."

"And how would you know?" Sam retorted. "You were too busy wooing the Over-the-Hill Gang to notice anything."

"I noticed," said Caroline in that maddeningly calm fashion. "*He* didn't."

"Hah! I think you're—" Sam stopped in midsentence. She had spent four hours in O'Rourke's company and he hadn't flirted, teased, flattered, conned, or tried to seduce her in any way, shape, or form. They'd talked and laughed and traded war stories but the one thing they hadn't done was look at each other the way men and women often did. "You're right," she said at last, sinking lower in her seat. "One hundred percent right."

To Murphy O'Rourke she was nothing more than Sam the Sandwich Maker. How depressing.

SAM STOOD IN THE DOORWAY fifteen minutes later and waited while her father climbed up into his truck, started the engine, then disappeared down the quiet, tree-lined street. There had been some difficult times along the way, but Sam doubted she'd be where she was today if it hadn't been for the unswerving love and support of her parents. It was thanks to them she had the house she lived in. If she could provide one-half of that solid foundation for Patty, she'd count her lucky stars.

Yawning, she stepped back inside and locked the door behind her. Of course, it would be wonderful if she'd been able to provide a father for her brilliant little girl, as well, but some things not even an eternal optimist like Sam could manage. She believed fervently in the importance of a stable home and strong family and knew that it was within her power to provide that for Patty. With her parents' help and Caroline's unstinting support, Sam had managed to keep a half step ahead of her daughter's growing needs.

At least, so far she had.

She tiptoed through the narrow hallway and inched open Patty's bedroom door. The little girl was asleep, her red hair unbraided and pulled into a ponytail atop her head. Her glasses rested on the nightstand next to a pitcher of water, a humidifier and a Mickey Mouse alarm clock that had been a present for her fourth birthday. Sam knelt down alongside the bed and pressed her lips carefully against her daughter's cheek and brow. Cool and dry, thank God. Her nostrils twitched at the smell of Vick's Vapo-Rub and she remembered many winter nights when she was the little girl in the bed with her own mother slipping into her room to check her progress.

Oh, she could give Patty love and tender care. She could give Patty support and encouragement and an extended family to lean on when the going got tough. Sam could give her child all those wonderful things that matter so much in the scheme of things. But Patty wasn't your average child and some of the things she needed went far beyond what Sam was able to provide—at least, right now. Princeton offered limitless opportunities for Patty to excel but the door to those opportunities was closed as tightly for Patty as they had been to Sam years ago. Money would open those doors and Sam aimed to earn enough to do so.

She placed a kiss on Patty's cool forehead then slipped from the room. For a moment she hesitated, forgetting her promise to her mother, and was sorely tempted to go back into the kitchen and dive into preparing some of the delicacies she had in store for the men of O'Rourke's Bar and Grill. She'd been running on adrenaline all evening and could more than likely put in a few good hours at the stove but the lure of a warm bath on a cold winter's night was too seductive to resist.

How wonderful it would be if she had *Bal à Versailles* to perfume the water and French soaps and candles twinkling next to the tub as she sipped a glass of wine. She ruefully watched her reflection in the bathroom mirror as she stripped out of her slacks and sweater. How wonderful it would be if she had black lace underwear to replace her sturdy white cotton briefs. How wonderful it would be if her dark hair shimmered with auburn highlights and curved rather than hung straight to the middle of her back.

Sighing, she settled into the warm water and rested her head against an inflatable bath pillow. No wonder Murphy O'Rourke thought of her as Sam the Sandwich Maker. Who could blame him? She was tall and skinny and as plain as a loaf of bread on a super-market shelf. Anything she'd ever known about makeup and hairstyles and perfume had disappeared along with the notion of spare time. Sam was a mother and a home owner; she was a student and an entre-preneur and a daughter and a best friend. But a woman, a lacy-lingerie-full-eye-makeup-French-perfume type of woman? Sam wouldn't know where to begin.

Interest in that type of thing had disappeared along with her Christmas spirit quite a few years back, and Sam simply didn't have the time or the energy to try to recapture either one.

If her daughter were to achieve her full potential, Fast Foods for the Fast Lane had to get off to a run-ning start with the New Year. There wasn't room in Sam's master plan for failure—not for her and not for her little girl. When Ronald Donovan walked out on her eleven Christmases ago, he'd left behind a very scared—and definitely pregnant—girl. Well, times had changed. Sam wasn't a girl any longer and she defi-nitely wasn't scared. She had Patty and she had her dream and all she had to do was survive one more Christmas and she'd be on her way to securing her lit-tle girl's future and her own in the bargain.

Everything else would simply have to wait.

Chapter Seven

From the first moment Patty's eyes opened the next morning, she knew it was going to be a special day. Her throat didn't hurt and her eyes didn't burn. She wasn't coughing or sneezing or blowing her nose.

And best of all, it was nine o'clock on a Wednesday morning and she could hear her mom whistling an old Beatles song in the kitchen! Patty sat up and sniffed the air as she donned her glasses. Bacon, French toast, and hot chocolate. She tossed off the blankets and swung her legs out of the bed, searching the cold oak floor for her slippers then slipping her feet inside. Grabbing her robe, she jumped up and hurried into the kitchen.

It had been a long time since she and her mom had had time together right in the middle of a regular week and Patty didn't want to miss a single second.

"Just in time," said Sam, as Patty hugged her around the waist. "If the bacon didn't work, I was going to put hot chocolate in your vaporizer."

"I'm all better." Patty stood still while her mother pressed the back of her hand to Patty's forehead. "See?"

"You're staying in today, just to be on the safe side."

Grinning, Patty took her seat at the kitchen table and reached for her glass of orange juice. "I smell garlic and tomatoes."

"I've trained you well." Sam placed a plate of French toast and crisp Canadian bacon in front of Patty. "That's for your friend Murphy and his pals. I'll be taking their trays of food over at noon."

Patty's heart bounced from one side of her chest to the other. Just thinking about the possibilities made her dizzy with excitement. She took a sip of juice then looked over at her mother. "Did you have fun with Aunt Caroline last night?"

"We did." Sam sat down opposite Patty and poured herself a cup of coffee.

"Did you eat at the Pizza Hut?"

"Nope. We ended up at the bar."

Patty thought she'd fall off her chair in surprise. "You ate dinner at the bar? I thought they didn't have a cook."

Sam gestured toward the pots simmering on her six-burner stove. "They don't. Murphy ordered in pizza with the works for everyone." She overlooked the fact that they had eaten theirs in a more private setting. No sense raising Patty's hopes.

"Wow!" Patty breathed.

"Don't go getting excited, kiddo." Her mom reached over and ruffled Patty's bangs. "We're talking pepperoni pizzas for twelve, not a candlelight dinner for two."

Patty speared a slice of bacon with her fork. "It's a start," she mumbled.

"Look at me, honey."

Reluctantly Patty met her mother's eyes and she didn't like what she saw there one bit. Why did her mother have to be so darned stubborn about these things? Murphy O'Rourke was absolutely perfect. Even Aunt Caroline thought so, and that was before she'd even met him. "What?" she asked, knowing she sounded just like a spoiled little kid.

"It wouldn't matter if I fell head over heels for Murphy."

"I don't understand."

"Honey, I'm just not his type."

"I still don't understand." Her mom might not be glamorous but she was definitely pretty. Okay, maybe she didn't fill out a T-shirt the same way that Aunt Caroline did, but *Cosmo* said all men didn't like women with chests like overstuffed sofa cushions.

"Maybe I can explain." Both Patty and her mom swiveled around in their chairs in time to see Caroline stroll into the cozy kitchen.

"I didn't hear you ring the doorbell," said Sam as Caroline joined them at the table.

Caroline grabbed an empty cup and reached for the coffeepot. "The door was open."

Her mom muttered something about changing the locks but Patty and her aunt only laughed.

"Your mom was right, Patricia," said Caroline, picking up the conversational ball. "She isn't Murphy O'Rourke's type at all."

Patty felt her mouth drop open in surprise. "But, I—"

Her aunt's dark blond brows lifted a fraction of an inch. "You should have seen them together last night—they could have been brother and sister."

For one long and scary moment Patty was afraid she would burst into tears like a big, fat baby, but just as her eyes were filling to the danger point, she caught the briefest smile flash over her aunt's face and her breath stopped. There was still a chance!

Caroline leaned forward, her eyes never leaving Patty. "You understand about chemistry, don't you?"

"Sure," said Patty, shrugging. "Like between Sam and Diane on *Cheers* and Maddie and Dave on *Moonlighting*."

"Exactly," said Caroline. "When it's there, everyone knows about it and when it's not—" she paused dramatically "—well, when it's not, there's nothing on earth you can do to fake it."

"Oh, for heaven's sake!" Sam scraped her chair back and stood up. "I'm going down to the basement for supplies. I hope you'll be through with this nonsense when I come back upstairs."

She fairly bristled with annoyance, and Patty had to bite the inside of her cheek to keep from shouting "Hooray!" Reverse child psychology. How clever of her aunt to think of it.

Caroline turned innocent blue eyes on Patty's mom. "Whatever has gotten into you, Samantha?" she inquired sweetly. "It isn't like you're interested in Mr. O'Rourke, is it?"

"No," said Sam, a bit too quickly to Patty's practiced ear. "I'm just tired of being the topic of discussion around here. Why don't you two try to find *you* a husband, Caroline? That might be fun."

With that, Patty's mother stormed out of the kitchen, muttering something about eye shadow damaging brain cells.

"You were right," said Caroline the moment Sam was out of earshot. "They're so wrong for each other that they're perfect."

"Isn't he wonderful?" asked Patty dreamily.

Caroline's chuckle was warm and amused. "Well, he's not my particular cup of tea but he *is* wonderful, I'll grant you that."

"Do you think they like each other?"

"They were thick as thieves last night. Even sneaked out together for a while. They seemed like old friends."

"They did? Wow!" breathed Patty, her pulse racing. "Did they kiss?"

"No," said Caroline, wrinkling her nose. "In fact, I'm not even certain they realize they're the opposite sex. At least not yet."

Patty slumped back in her seat. "Then I don't understand, Aunt Caroline. You said they were—"

"Perfect for each other." She gave Patty's earlobes an affectionate tug. "You know it. I know it. It's just a question of getting them to know it."

Knowing about sexual chemistry and understanding it were two different things. It was easier to understand quantum physics then to understand why grownups acted the way they did. "Can't friends get married?" It seemed to Patty it would be a whole lot easier to spend fifty years with someone you actually liked being around and not just someone you liked to kiss.

Patty struggled with the concept, but her view of romance was limited to movie images of beautiful Technicolor people in beautiful Technicolor costumes. How romance would find her sweater-and-jeans mother was a puzzlement. Suddenly she brightened. "Is it like icing on a cake?"

"Yes!" Caroline's smile was brilliant. "The cake is just fine without the icing but what a difference it makes when you have it."

"But we still have to get them together, don't we?" Apparently making sandwiches was a good ice-breaker, but it wasn't about to thaw a glacier like Sam.

"Easy!" Caroline snapped her fingers. "The Christmas Masquerade Ball."

"You know Mom hates parties even more than she hates Christmas. She'll never go."

"Deep down old Scrooge loves Christmas, Patricia, and she loves parties. She just keeps herself too busy to realize it."

"I don't know," said Patty, feeling extremely skeptical. "If she didn't have me, I think she'd pretend the whole thing didn't exist."

"Trust me, sweetie—under all that bluster, your mom is an old yuletide cheerleader from way back. She used to start counting the days before Christmas back around Labor Day."

Patty had to laugh at the thought of her sobersides mother keeping a Christmas countdown, but then she grew serious. "It's all because of my real dad, isn't it, the reason she doesn't like Christmas?"

Aunt Caroline was one of those rare adults who believed in being honest with kids, even if it wasn't always exactly what you wanted to hear. "Yes, that's how it started, Patricia, but that isn't all of it. The trouble now is she's been running so hard, for such a long time, that she's forgotten everything she used to know about fun.''

''She's forgotten about Christmas?''

''She's forgotten everything that's good about it.''

Imagine needing to remember how to enjoy Christmas. Being grownup didn't seem so wonderful to Patty when she heard things like that.

''She'll never go to the ball,'' said Patty firmly. ''Never.''

''She'll go,'' said Caroline.

''She can't afford it.''

''She won't have to.''

''She'll say she has nothing to wear.''

''When her best friend owns a rent-a-dress shop? She'll never get away with that.''

''What if Murphy O'Rourke doesn't go?'' Somehow it was easier to imagine him ringside at an Atlantic City boxing match than fluttering around a dance floor dressed like a penguin in a tuxedo.

''Believe me, there's nothing to worry about.''

Patty listened to her aunt's scheme to get Sam to the masquerade ball with growing delight.

''And if it doesn't work?'' she asked Caroline when her aunt was finished speaking. ''What then?''

Caroline turned her graceful hands, palms up, on the tabletop. ''If it doesn't work, we sit back and let nature take its course. I don't think we have anything to worry about.''

Sam's footsteps clattered up the basement steps and Patty gasped as Sam entered the room. Her mother's straight dark hair was swirled on top of her head in soft curls. A diamond tiara glittered amidst the silky tendrils. She wore a shimmering gown of sapphire satin that bared her shoulders and fit closely at the waist, then billowed out into a luxuriously full skirt that reached to the floor. Only the toes of her sparkly pumps were visible. Her mom wore makeup and lipstick, mascara and blush, and at her ears the largest pair of diamonds Patty had ever seen twinkled for all the world to see.

It was a miracle!

Patty blinked once, then twice.

It was a dream.

There stood her mother in her everyday jeans and sweater, her dark hair long about her narrow shoulders, her arms piled high with cans of whole tomatos and puree.

"Patty?" Sam asked, heading for the counter across the room. "Is something wrong?"

Patty shook her head and looked over at her aunt Caroline whose smile held a few surprises of its own.

"We can't miss!" mouthed her aunt and Patty prayed she was right because in less than seventy-two hours, the great makeover of Samantha Elizabeth Dean was set to begin.

YOU KNEW western civilization was coming to a bad end when men like Murphy O'Rourke and Dan Stein held business meetings over scrambled eggs, bagels and coffee-with-cream-two-sugars-make-it-decaf-would-ya-honey.

The waitress scratched her head with the eraser end of her pencil and sashayed back to the kitchen of the

Colonial Diner on Route 1 as Murphy prepared to do battle.

"Okay, Dan, now that you've blasted hell out of your expense account, I'll cut to the bottom line—you're wasting your time."

Dan, sixty-two years old and sixty-two pounds over his fighting weight, glared at O'Rourke and lit up a Camel. "It's my time to waste. We want you back, kid, and we're willing to spend big bucks to get you."

Murphy looked around at the red vinyl and white formica interior of the diner and guffawed. "Yeah, Dan. You're pulling out all the stops, aren't you?"

Dan grinned around his cigarette. "What's the matter kid—you got something against a power breakfast?"

"Somehow I don't think this qualifies."

"Hey, you take what you can get in this world. If I could get you out of this godforsaken backwater burg, I'd show you something that'd knock your eyes out." Dan took a long drag on his cigarette. "You do remember how to get to Manhattan, don't you?"

"All too well," muttered Murphy as the waitress deposited their coffee and orange juice. "Gimme another month or two and I might be able to forget it."

"You and your old man still at each other's throats?"

"So what else is new?" Murphy gulped down his oj. "Thirty-six years and counting. We're going for the North American record."

"How's he doing?" Dan Stein and Bill O'Rourke were the same age and had similar medical histories.

"Pretty good. He should be back behind the bar by the middle of January, give or take a few weeks."

Dan narrowed his eyes and gave Murphy his best managing editor's scowl. "You plannin' on going into business with the guy?"

Murphy groaned and leaned back in his booth. The red vinyl seat crackled with the movement. "One of us would be up for murder-one within a week."

"You goin' on unemployment?"

"Can it, will you, Stein. You're giving me indigestion."

"You're gonna get more than indigestion when I tell you the big boss is gettin' tired of waiting for you to come to your senses."

Murphy bit into his bagel with gusto. "Gianelli should've thought of that when we had the fight."

"You were out of line."

"The hell I was." Murphy and the publisher of the *New York Telegram* had butted heads over newspaper policy. Frank Gianelli had hired Murphy away from the foreign beat with promises of free license to explore the domestic political scene, only to turn the *Telegram* into a cross between the *National Enquirer* and the Morton Downey television show.

"He's willing to give in on a few issues."

"He knows my number. Let him call me."

"He's a proud man."

"So am I."

"He's also a stubborn man."

"So am I."

Dan drained his coffee cup and flagged down the waitress for a refill. "You've got yourself a safety net, haven't you?"

Murphy grinned. "Am I that transparent?"

"You jumping back on the foreign beat?"

"I've got some feelers out."

"I thought you'd had enough of living out of a suitcase."

"So had I." A few weeks back in New Jersey with his father had shown Murphy that while family unity was possible for some people, it wasn't possible for the O'Rourkes. His brother could make a phone call once a month and be praised to the skies. Murphy could roll up his sleeves and take over the bar and be ignored. "Let's say I've had enough of domestic tranquility to last me awhile."

When in doubt, hit the road. It seemed as good a way as any to cope with life.

Dan lit up another cigarette. "I think you can get what you want out of Gianelli if you'll meet him halfway."

"Not interested."

"We're talking long-term career move here, O'Rourke, not just a two-year gig in Paris."

"Don't knock what you haven't tried, Dan. Those two-year gigs in Paris make for some nice memories."

"Memories don't keep you warm in your old age."

Murphy arched a brow. "Oh, yeah?"

"Why shouldn't you settle down and pay off a mortgage like the rest of us?"

"If I could find a woman like Marion, I just might."

Dan threw his head back and laughed his husky smoker's laugh. "Find your own woman, O'Rourke. It's taken me forty years to get used to the one I've got."

Envy, white-hot and unexpected, flared deep in Murphy's gut. Thirty-year mortgages and forty-year marriages. Kids and college tuition. Graduation, weddings, christenings. The whole normal chain of events.

He didn't know a damn thing about any of it and probably never would.

Dan looked longingly at a stack of pancakes on the table across the way. "Think we talked enough business to satisfy the IRS?"

"I think so."

"You'll consider Gianelli's offer?"

Murphy nodded.

"How about some pancakes?"

Murphy grinned and flagged down the exhausted waitress. "I thought you'd never ask."

OVERNIGHT huge candy canes and strings of lights and plastic manger scenes had sprouted on every lawn and store Sam passed on her way to O'Rourke's Bar and Grill, as if Santa Claus had himself declared Christmas decorations mandatory in New Jersey. A giant elf, sporting a green costume and pointy-toed slippers with bells on the toes, stood in front of Ben's Hardware Store and waved at traffic. He looked suspiciously like the accountant who'd danced attendance on Caroline at her last soiree.

Christmas. What a bizarre time of year. Perfectly sane human beings did the strangest things. Sam pulled her Blazer into the parking lot of O'Rourke's Bar and Grill at one minute to noon.

"Murphy?" she called out as she entered the dimly lit bar. "It's Sam, Murphy!"

No answer. How strange. She put the tray down atop one of the wooden tables and glanced about. A camel's hair coat was draped over a chair. Maybe Murphy was in the tiny room behind the kitchen that served as an office.

Well, no matter. She'd finish unloading the Blazer first, then go searching for him.

Sam turned and headed for the door when Scotty's cheerful voice stopped her.

"Greetings, Samantha," he said, his intelligent face lit with a pleasant smile. "What wonders have you wrought this fine day?"

"No fair, Scotty! You'll have to wait and see."

He sniffed the air speculatively. "Do I smell Danish ham and sweet gherkins on cocktail rye with a soupçon of Dijon mustard for tang?"

"It looks like I'll have my work cut out for me if I want to keep you surprised."

"Don't worry about him," came a voice from the entrance. "It's the boss you should be worrying about."

Both Sam and Scotty turned to see Murphy O'Rourke, arms piled high with boxes, kick the door shut after him.

"Where do you want these?" Murphy pretended to stagger beneath the load of food.

Sam stepped forward to help him. "Let me take this—"

He grunted something and moved past her. "Just point out a place, why don't you?"

Sam pointed to the table where she'd placed the first tray. "Right over there."

"We're going to have to renegotiate the price, Dean." O'Rourke's countenance was fierce. "There's a hell of a lot of food here."

Sam's back went up in defense. "Don't worry, O'Rourke. The extras are on the house."

"No way."

Her eyes widened in surprise. "I thought you were feeling ripped off."

"You're the one who should be feeling ripped off. You contracted to make sandwiches, not five-course meals."

"Consider it a rehearsal for my opening in January. I'm trying to perfect my techniques. Why let all these goodies go to waste?" True enough. There was a limit to how much she and Patty could consume, and besides, after the killer deal her daughter put together, she felt she owed O'Rourke and his clientele a few extras.

Scotty turned toward Murphy who was shrugging his way out of a leather bomber jacket. "How was your power breakfast?"

Murphy started to say something then glanced at Sam and caught himself. "In polite words, lousy."

Scotty, a gentleman to the tips of his manicured fingers, turned to include Sam in the conversation. "Our mutual friend's employer—"

"Former employer," grunted Murphy.

Scotty winked at Sam and continued, "His former employer saw fit to travel all the way from the city—"

"There's a big deal," said Murphy, tying on his apron. "All of sixty miles. The man will do anything to get out of Manhattan."

"His former employer came all the way from the city to talk to this pigheaded young man about furthering his career."

"What career? I'm a bartender now."

"Murphy has the opportunity to become managing editor of the *New York Telegram*."

Sam turned to Murphy, who was busy stomping around the bar with the subtlety of a wounded buffalo. "Managing editor. I'm impressed."

"Don't be," said Murphy.

"He's in a snit," continued Scotty, unperturbed. "He longs for the life of the foreign correspondent."

Of course he would, thought Sam. If ever a man looked ready to run, it was Murphy O'Rourke.

"The offers aren't exactly pouring in." Murphy's tone was gruff. "Apparently my time has come and gone."

It was an oddly vulnerable remark from a man who seemed invulnerable to such things as insecurity, but there it was. Sam found she liked Murphy O'Rourke more than ever.

"I think you have a few good years left in you," she said lightly, touching his forearm. "I wouldn't worry about it."

"You're a kid," said Murphy with a sudden twinkle in his hazel eyes. "What would you know about it?"

"I'm twenty-eight, and I know more than you realize."

"Talk to me when you're on the downside of thirty-five. It's a whole other world."

"It's what you make of it," said Sam, "no matter what age you are."

"Bravo!" Scotty, who had been listening to their exchange, broke into spirited applause. "Give this woman a drink on the house."

Sam laughed and shook her head. "I'll take a rain check. I have work to do at my shop."

"How about coffee and a sandwich?" Murphy inclined his head toward the trays resting upon the table. "I hear our caterer does a damn good job."

"She's the best in the business," said Sam, "even if nobody's ever heard of her."

"That will change soon enough." He pulled out a chair and motioned her toward it. "I'll bet you didn't eat breakfast."

"I made french toast, bacon, and hot chocolate."

"Yeah," he said with an answering grin, "but how much of it did you manage to get?"

"Would you believe black coffee and a sip of juice?"

"I'd believe it. Like I said, you're too skinny."

Sam shrugged and reached for a sliced chicken and tomato sandwich with dilled mayonnaise on pumpernickel. "I can see when I'm outnumbered. Are you gentlemen going to join me?"

Murphy grabbed the sandwich closest to him while Scotty searched out the Danish ham he'd zeroed in on when Sam arrived. Munching on his sandwich, he carried a pot of strong black coffee over to their table and pulled a container of cream from the small refrigerator behind the bar. Sam threw her cholesterol count to the wind and helped herself.

"The folly of youth," said Scotty with an envious sigh. "I remember the days when milk and cream and eggs were good for you."

"Don't remind me," Sam moaned. "Do you know how sad it is to have to turn out a reduced-fat, reduced-cholesterol, reduced-calorie version of beef stroganoff?"

"The only thing sadder is having to eat it," said Murphy, straddling the chair next to her. "Smoking's no good for you. Sugar can kill." He shot Sam a look. "Even sex isn't what it used to be."

"Speak for yourself," said MacTavish.

Sam nibbled on her sandwich and watched O'Rourke out of the corner of her eye. So sex wasn't what it used to be, hmm? Wouldn't she love to know the story behind *that* statement.

A charged silence filled the room and Scotty—bless him—jumped in.

"The average English high tea has probably lined the pockets of more cardiologists and dentists than a lifetime of steak dinners."

Murphy laughed but Sam could only sigh.

"High tea," she said dreamily. "What I wouldn't give for one afternoon at Claridge's."

Once again she found herself under Murphy's professional scrutiny. "You've never been to Europe?"

"I've never been anywhere," she said matter-of-factly. "I've gone as far east as Manhattan and as far west as Philadelphia."

"New Jersey born and bred?"

She nodded. "I can see my epitaph—'Here lies Samantha Dean, she lived and died in Rocky Hill and never knew the difference.'" The words were out before she could stop them and the biting edge to her tone of voice surprised herself as much as it surprised the two men. "Sorry. I didn't mean to sound like that. I'm actually very happy here."

"There is no crime in craving travel, my dear," said Scotty kindly. "It is a natural desire of the active mind."

"It's one of the reasons I became a foreign correspondent," said Murphy as he poured them all more coffee. "I wanted to get out of here more than I wanted anything else on earth."

"When I was sixteen I used to lie awake nights, dreaming of London and Paris and Rome and all of the other wonderful places that were waiting for me to discover them." She had also lain awake nights, dreaming of how wonderful it would be to see those glorious places with Ronald Donovan. Her dreams of Ronald were long over but she was pierced with a sudden, bittersweet yearning for all the other foolish dreams that had once seemed so important.

"And then you had Patty?" asked Scotty.

"Yes. And then I had Patty. Not even London could compete with that."

"You could still go," said Murphy. "Kids are portable."

How could she explain to the footloose O'Rourke that while kids were portable, she wasn't. Years ago she'd made up her mind to stay put and, despite this outburst, she did not regret her decision. Travel took both time and money, and at the moment both commodities were tied up in Fast Foods for the Fast Lane. "Who knows?" she said after a moment. "Maybe someday I'll get there."

"Go," said Murphy. "You owe it to yourself to see England."

"Yes," said Sam, "but I owe it to Patty to stay here." Patty needed continuity; she needed security and challenges and every single cent Sam could possibly spare for her future education. Trips to London, no matter how wonderful, were dreams for some distant future when Sam was a successful entrepreneur and Murphy O'Rourke was just a topic of conversation around the bar.

O'Rourke didn't say anything. He nodded his head slowly, his gaze never leaving hers. In his eyes she saw something close to respect and admiration. And even though his opinion shouldn't have mattered, her heart beat just a little bit faster.

Chapter Eight

Murphy wasn't quite sure how it happened, but by the time three o'clock rolled around, he was in one bear of a bad mood. Scotty, Joe and the rest of the crowd had taken a tray of sandwiches and a pile of appetizers and retired to a table near the exit. From time to time they cast such baleful looks at him that Murphy almost felt contrite.

Almost, but not quite.

He never should have let Dan Stein talk him into that little "power" breakfast at the diner. That had been a lousy idea from the word go, and if Murphy'd had half a brain, he wouldn't have given the die-hard New Yorker directions to Rocky Hill. Born and bred New Yorkers didn't believe there was actually life on the other side of the Hudson River; if Murphy'd used his head, he would have let Stein go on thinking exactly that. But, no. His damn curiosity had gotten the better of him and Murphy let himself be coerced into consorting with the enemy.

All he had to do was say no to the *Telegram*'s offer and mean it. Sounded simple enough. Why was he finding it so hard to stick with his decision? In any given day he found himself vacillating between the life of a foreign correspondent, going back to Manhattan and the *Telegram* and disconnecting his word processor and pulling draft beer for the rest of his days.

Talking to Samantha Dean, listening to her optimism about her future and that of her daughter, made him aware of a void inside himself that he hadn't known was there until that moment. Sam knew who she was, and what she was about. She understood where she was going, how to get there and what was expected of her once she arrived. And add to all that the awesome responsibility of a child with a potential as phenomenal as Patty's, and you had a woman who was pretty phenomenal in her own right.

In one day Sam Dean did more that was important than Murphy O'Rourke had done in his entire life, a fact his father had been more than happy to point out after Sam left for her shop. Bill O'Rourke had come in from his morning constitutional and taken an immediate shine to the friendly young woman. It had been a long time since Murphy had seen a genuine smile on his dour father's face but Sam Dean had managed to call forth not only a smile but an actual laugh, as well. Scotty told Murphy that it had taken all of his willpower to keep from leading the patrons of the bar in a loud "Hip hip hooray!"

Bill's smile had faded the moment Sam left for her shop, and before she backed her Blazer out of the parking lot, Murphy and his old man were engaged in one of their sniping sessions. Bill stormed up to his room to nap. Murphy stormed about the bar, bullying the regulars and eating enough for six fullbacks after a famine.

"Retirement is supposed to be a time of fulfillment and tranquility," observed Scotty as Murphy clattered glassware and trays behind the bar. "Your foul disposition makes me long for the halls of academe once again."

"Be my guest," said Murphy, glaring at the former mathematics professor. "I'll drive you."

"Why don't you go out and take a walk?"

Murphy glanced toward the window. "It's snowing out there."

"It might cool you off."

"I don't need to cool off."

"That, my boy, is a matter of opinion. I think you need a change of venue."

Murphy glanced at the empty sandwich trays stacked at the far end of the bar. "Maybe that's not such a bad idea."

"The walk?" asked Scotty.

"No. The change of venue."

"But you just said—"

"When you're right, you're right, Scotty." He untied his apron and tossed it near the sink. "Can you watch things for me while I'm gone?"

Scotty cast a scornful look at the ancient cash register and the beer mugs waiting to be filled. "I think the time has come to talk about putting me on the payroll. I am highly overqualified for this work."

"You're a pal, Scotty. I won't be long."

He grabbed his leather jacket, his car keys and the metal trays. Why not? he thought, as he headed across the snowy parking lot toward his rented car. She'd been knocking herself out these past few days making epicurean delights for the guys at the bar. She must have her hands full with Patty home sick and Christmas coming and getting her store ready to open in less than a month.

The least he could do was stop by Fast Foods for the Fast Lane, drop off the trays and save her a trip back to O'Rourke's that night.

It doesn't mean anything, he thought as he started the car and cautiously eased the vehicle out onto the slippery street. If he didn't get out of the bar for a while he'd probably deplete a month's worth of Scotch before the afternoon was out.

He slid to an off-angle stop at a traffic light. Damn weather. She didn't need to be out in it, risking her life. She had a daughter who needed her, family and friends who cared. He could imagine her with a husband and a few more kids with Patty's brains and her smile. Murphy grunted as he moved the car forward again. Nobody'd notice if he plowed into a snowdrift and stayed there until spring.

You're a coward, son. He heard his father's voice as clearly as if he were in the car alongside him. *Anytime life doesn't go your way, you're looking to back out.*

"Can you blame me?" he mumbled, his fingers gripping the wheel as the snow thickened. "Who wants to spend winter in New Jersey?"

He thought of Samantha Dean and a smile broke through his foul mood. He liked her. Nothing complicated about that. He liked her ambition, her devotion to her daughter, her straightforward manner and her offbeat sense of humor.

When he was seventeen he was a wiseacre kid with more bravado than brains.

When Sam was seventeen, she was a senior in high school—and the mother of a newborn baby girl.

Murphy couldn't imagine what a hash he would have made of a situation like that.

It didn't take a genius to know Sam was something pretty special. He enjoyed her company as much as he had enjoyed her daughter's at the Career Day seminar at the grammar school. He'd never given a lot of thought to having a woman for a friend before. Reporters in general, and foreign correspondents in particular, weren't known for their fidelity to members of the opposite sex. The life-style wasn't exactly conducive to forging lifetime commitments and Murphy hadn't been overly interested in finding an alternative. His one brief shot at marriage had been over before it had a chance to begin, and frankly he hadn't been devastated by the divorce.

He and his wife had been lovers but they'd never been friends. In fact, there had been a lot of women he'd enjoyed in bed but few he'd ever tried to enjoy once they got out. He and Sam were off to a good start, and for some reason that made him feel better than he had in a long, long time.

SAM HAD JUST FINISHED sealing twenty pounds of unbleached flour into two huge metal canisters and was about to arrange her spices in alphabetical order on the open shelves near the stove when she heard a knock at the front door.

"Sorry," she called out, pushing her hair off her face with the back of her hand, "we're not open yet."

The knock sounded again.

"We're closed! Come back New Year's Day."

"Sam! Open up."

She stopped and stared toward the front of the store. Murphy O'Rourke? "What are you doing here?" she asked as she ushered the snow-covered man inside and relocked the door. "How on earth did you find me?"

He presented the empty trays to her with a flourish. "I wanted to save you a trip," he said, brushing the snow off his hair with a quick shake of his head, "and it wasn't too hard."

"You reporter types are resourceful."

He glanced around the bright and airy storefront and whistled low. "You entrepreneur types are pretty resourceful yourself."

Sam beamed with pleasure. "Thanks, Murphy. It *is* shaping up pretty nicely."

"Nicely? This place is dynamite. You'll be turning the yuppies away in droves."

Her laughter was high and unforced. "That's the general idea." In the distance they heard the low rumble of a New Jersey Transit train pulling into the Princeton Junction station. "Some location, isn't it? They fall out of the train, tired and hungry, and into my shop to pick up their dinner."

He folded his brawny arms across his chest and nodded. "I have to hand it to you, Sam, you covered all the angles. I don't see how you can miss."

Sam crossed herself and grinned like a kid caught in the cookie jar. "From your mouth to God's ear. Unless I've missed my guess, Fast Foods for the Fast Lane is just what Mr. and Ms Commuter are looking for." Suddenly she realized she was clutching the empty food trays to her chest like a shield. "You didn't have to do this, you know. I was going to stop at the bar on my way home."

"I figured I'd save you a trip."

She nodded as she placed the trays down atop the Corian counter that had cost her an arm and a leg on sale. "And I suppose you just happened to be in the neighborhood."

His hazel eyes twinkled. "No," he said. "I wasn't anywhere close and I'll have you know, the only thing I hate more than driving, is driving in a snowstorm."

She ducked her head for a moment, feeling inordinately pleased that someone would go out of his way to be in her company. It had been a long time since she'd felt particularly likable and the sensation was as delightful as it was noteworthy. "The least I can do is give you the grand tour."

"Wait a minute," he said, turning up the collar of his jacket. "I have to get something from the car."

He was back in a flash, brandishing a snow-covered, but absolutely delightful, pot of Christmas cactus abloom with vivid pink flowers. A huge lump formed in Sam's throat.

"Murphy! I don't know what to say..."

"You don't have to say anything." He handed her the beautiful plant. "Good luck with your shop."

She buried her face in the blossoms, taking those extra seconds to blink away sudden and surprising tears. Composure regained, she cleared a spot on what would soon be her main counter.

"Looks good," said Murphy.

"It looks wonderful!" said Sam, wiping sawdust off the counter top. "I may rethink my color scheme."

"Don't go getting crazy. It's only a little plant, Sam."

"Yes," said Sam, meeting his eyes, "but it's special." She raised up on her toes and kissed his cheek. His after-shave was spicy and crisp and altogether appealing. "Thanks."

"So what about the grand tour you promised me?" He slipped off his leather jacket and draped it over a step stool near the massive chrome refrigerator. "As far as I can see, this is the whole shebang."

"My dear Mr. O'Rourke, this is only the merest hint of the wonders inside this shop." Sam gave him her best number-one-businesswoman look. "Why, you haven't even seen my stove yet."

"What are you waiting for?" He grinned and took her arm. "Lead the way."

There was really nothing all that special about a restaurant-size stove or an industrial-strength microwave but to Sam they were as thrilling as a brand-new, shiny red Porsche. At best her acquisitions had elicited no more than pleasant smiles from her family and friends, and she had expected no more than perfunctory courtesy from Murphy.

She was wrong.

"Will you look at these shelves?" he said when he swung open the double doors to the refrigerator and stuck his head inside. "You could fit three Thanksgiving turkeys in here and still have room for a side of beef."

The stove was greeted with a low whistle, followed by a thorough inspection of the center griddle, the warming oven, and all six burners. "Pilotless?" he asked as he fiddled with a dial.

"Of course," said Sam. "This is a first-rate outfit I'm running here."

He duly noted the wattage of the microwave, the water temperature of her dishwasher, and the beautiful baking pans that had cost her more than a sane person would have paid for them. She found herself eager to show him every nook and cranny of the kitchen, displaying her dazzling array of takeout containers before him as if they were a king's ransom in emeralds.

She couldn't remember the last time she had felt so exhilarated and confident over her prospects—or quite so happy to share them with a friend.

"I have to hand it to you," Sam said ten minutes later over coffee in the front room, where she could cast quick peeks at her beautiful Christmas cactus. "Not only did you suffer through the grand tour, you actually asked questions!"

"Reporter's training." O'Rourke popped a peanut into his mouth and took another gulp of coffee. "I'm always looking for a good story."

"Well, this is the one," said Sam proudly. "Mark my words—I'm going to make my name or know the reason why."

"I believe you."

She looked him straight in the eye, and to her surprise he didn't blink. "I think you really do."

She told him about her plans for Fast Foods, about the delivery service, and the FAX machine for jet-age orders, and the way she hoped to provide a superlative product and still make a superlative profit.

"A practical dreamer," said O'Rourke when she finally paused for a breath. "I never thought I'd meet one."

"What about you?" she asked. "Are you a dreamer, too?"

"Me?" His laugh was brittle. "I gave up dreaming a hell of a long time ago, Sam."

"I don't believe you," she said, touching his wrist then pulling away, embarrassed by her boldness. "I see it in your eyes."

"You're seeing too many years of sleepless nights, that's all."

Let it go, Sam. This isn't your business. O'Rourke was a rare find: a man who actually listened. Why not be satisfied with that and not expect him to unburden himself like a guest on Oprah or Phil Donahue. She cast about for a new topic of conversation. "How are you at installing water faucets?"

"Don't know the first thing about it." It was the cheerful admission of a man who didn't need to know and was glad of the fact.

She pushed her chair away from the table and stood up. "How would you feel about holding the flashlight for me?"

He pushed his chair away from the table and stood up across from her. "I think I can manage it."

"Come on," said Sam, heading for the kitchen. "I'll put you to work."

Two and a half hours later Sam had the faucets working, the garbage disposal running, and—thanks to Murphy—five perfectly matched utility shelves hanging proudly over her butcher-block worktable.

"You have hidden talents," she said, as she admired their handiwork. "You should have been a carpenter."

"It may come to that yet." His tone was jovial but she caught an undercurrent of anxiety.

"Don't worry," she said, in her best mother-knows-best manner. "You'll be back on the foreign beat before you know it."

He moved in front of her, hands on his hips, head cocked to the side. "Yeah?"

"Yeah. You're too good to stay unemployed for long."

"How would you know? You haven't read a damn word I've written."

"Call it feminine intuition," said Sam over his loud groan. "You wouldn't let yourself be anything but terrific."

He laughed and ruffled her hair the way she often ruffled Patty's and an oddly pleasant ripple of sensation tingled deep inside her stomach. "Come on, Sam. There's a blizzard out there. Let's hit the road."

Sam glanced out the plate-glass window and shivered. "Good grief! It really does look like a blizzard." She tossed Murphy his coat and grabbed for her own. "Beat you to my car."

They slipped and slid their way across the snowy driveway, their laughter mingling with the sound of tires spinning from the street beyond. The snow was already well past her ankles and Sam knew her slacks were headed for the rag bin but she didn't care as Murphy ducked behind his rented car and started to make a snowball.

"Throw that and you're a dead man, O'Rourke."
She dived behind her Blazer and began pressing
handfuls of snow into a big ball. "I have the best aim
in all of Mercer County."

Splat!

A huge wet snowball found its mark on Sam's right
shoulder.

Murphy, blast his hide, peered over the fender of his
car. "What was that about having the best aim in
Mercer County?"

She ducked as another snowball whizzed past her.

"Lucky shot!" Sam fell against the side of her
Blazer, sputtering and laughing. It was hard to talk
with a mouthful of snow.

"Give up?" called Murphy.

"Not on your life!" She scrambled behind the fender of her Blazer and went into overdrive as another
missile landed just over her head. "You won't get
away with this, O'Rourke!" In the blink of an eye she
had an arsenal of snowballs lined up and ready to go.
"Take this!" she called and fired one off in his direction.

The man was too smart for his own good and he
neatly deflected her shot. "Give up, Sam!" he said,
taking aim again. "No woman alive can **bea**t me."

It was her turn to duck. His snowball caught the
edge of her right shoulder. She remained undaunted,
pressed against the fender, snowball at the ready.

"What's the matter, Sam?" he called. "Running
out of steam already?"

The smug sound of male superiority had Sam seeing
red, but she kept quiet and still.

"Hey, Sam! Are you okay?"

Still Sam said nothing. She waited.

"I know what you're trying and it's not going to work. I wasn't all-star snowball thrower on the Geneva beat for nothing."

Silence. Sam could taste imminent victory and it was sweet.

"Sam?" Murphy's footsteps crunched across the parking lot. Closer...closer...

"Bull's-eye!" Sam's cry shattered the stillness and she roared with laughter at the look of surprise on Murphy's snow-covered face. "Never underestimate the power of a woman with a mission!"

Murphy sputtered and blinked and shook his head free of the splattered snowball.

"You play dirty," he said, his hazel eyes bright against his snowy lashes. "I never would've figured you for the type."

Sam flashed him a triumphant smile. "That'll teach you for typecasting people. I play to win."

"All's fair, etcetera, etcetera?"

"That's right." Sam was feeling quite smug.

"You're sure about that?"

"Positive."

The next instant Sam found herself swept up into Murphy's strong arms and deposited soundly into a snowdrift.

It was his turn to laugh. "All's fair, Sam," he said.

With that Sam grabbed him by the right calf and, praying her self-defense training wouldn't fail her, flipped him right off his feet.

And right on top of her!

"You're right," Sam said as his torso sprawled across her legs. "I *do* play dirty!"

The expression on Murphy's face was priceless. "I'll give you fifty dollars to keep this to yourself."

Sam knew her eyes were twinkling with delight. "I'll let you know."

"You could ruin my reputation at the bar if you tell the guys you bested me."

"Remember that, next time you start a snowball fight with a defenseless woman."

He leaned up on one elbow and met her eyes. His shaggy sandy-brown hair fell across his forehead, and his face was ruddy from the snow and the winter wind. He looked rumpled, healthy and, all in all, quite appealing. Sam was surprised at exactly *how* appealing.

"I like you, Samantha Dean." His voice held a note of admiration.

Again she experienced that odd fluttering sensation deep inside. "The feeling's mutual, Murphy O'Rourke."

They stumbled to their feet, laughing and dusting the snow off each other's clothing. O'Rourke seemed to take an inordinate pleasure in brushing her derriere clean and Sam made certain she got in an answering message of her own. Murphy waited while she climbed into her beat-up Blazer and started her engine.

"See you tomorrow," said Sam through the open window as the wind-driven snow swirled all about.

O'Rourke leaned inside and placed a kiss on her cheek. "See you tomorrow." The kiss was chaste, swift and almost brotherly.

Sam was very still as he plodded through the snow to his car and wondered what life would be like if she were a small and curvy blue-eyed blonde. The idea quickly disappeared, but the sweet warm feeling of his lips against her cheek lingered as Sam drove home through the storm.

PATTY COULDN'T EXPLAIN how she knew, but the moment she woke up on Thursday morning she would have bet her Pound Puppy that something had changed.

Her mom had been real quiet last night, not at all her usual chatty self. It wasn't that her mom was unhappy exactly; it was more like she had something on her mind and couldn't stop thinking about whatever it was.

And now, at eight o'clock on a snowy morning, her mom was *singing* in the kitchen. It wasn't just that she was singing, it was *what* she was singing. Patty leaped out of bed and pulled on her slippers and robe. She eased her door open and slipped down the hallway toward the kitchen. Her I-hate-Christmas mom was singing "Jingle Bells."

Patty stood in the doorway, transfixed with wonder. Murphy O'Rourke. It just had to be....

"Are you going to stand there all morning, kiddo, or would you like some breakfast?"

Patty started as she realized her mom was talking to her.

"You were singing Christmas carols," said Patty, staring at Sam as if she were an apparition.

"I don't think so, honey." Sam flipped the pancakes one-two.

"You were," Patty persisted. "I heard you with my own ears."

Sam shrugged and reached for a breakfast plate. "And what if I was? That's all you hear on the radio these days."

Patty poured herself a glass of orange juice and helped herself to a Flintstone vitamin. "Am I going to school today?"

"Look outside, kiddo. School's closed."

Patty walked over to the window and peered through the yellow and orange curtains. "Wow!" Her breath left a moist circle on the glass. "Can I go sledding with Susan?"

"And be home sick another two days? Not very likely."

"Maa-a-a." Patty sank into a kitchen chair. "I'm getting bored being stuck in the house." She'd already finished volumes one through five of the remaindered encyclopaedia her mom had found at the book store.

"Who said anything about staying in the house?" Sam deposited a stack of pancakes on the plate in front of Patty. "I thought you could come with me to the store."

"Yuk." Patty poured maple syrup on her pancakes. "There's nothing to do there."

"Oh, really?" Her mother sat down opposite her and frowned at the river of syrup pooling on Patty's plate. "I thought you could help me paint."

What a boring day! Patty couldn't remember why she'd ever thought something special might happen. She'd just as soon work on her mathematical equation that proved the existence of the Star of Bethlehem than paint walls. No television or radio or—

"Did you hear what I said, Patty?"

"We're going to paint the store," she said, sounding as glum as she felt.

"I asked if you wanted to stop at O'Rourke's with me when I drop off the food trays." Her mother took a sip of coffee. "I could use some help."

Patty wanted to jump on the table and dance with delight but her aunt Caroline's words sounded inside her head. *Be cool, Patricia. If Samantha figures out what we're up to, it's all over.* "I guess I'll go." Perfect! She sounded as if she'd rather stay home and mope.

"We'll be leaving in an hour. Do you think you can be ready?"

Patty looked down at her pancakes and struggled not to smile. "Yeah."

"You don't have to go, Patty. I can come back and pick you up before we go to the store."

"That's okay, Mom. I'll be ready."

Nothing in the world could keep Patty away from seeing her mother and future father together for the very first time.

Not even a blizzard!

"THAT'S SOME KID you've got there," said Murphy O'Rourke as he helped Sam arrange the sandwiches and appetizers on serving platters. "Scotty usually doesn't like anybody under thirty-five."

"Then that makes them even," Sam said, reassembling a triple-decker B.L.T. on white toast. "Patty doesn't, either."

Her little girl and the cultured professor had hit it off like a house afire. The moment they were introduced Patty launched into a discussion of higher mathematics that left everyone else in the bar gasping for air. When she explained a concept even Scotty didn't know about, he smiled and said he bowed to a higher intelligence.

"Let us find a table away from the masses," said Scotty with a wink in Sam's direction. "I want to hear your theory on exponential equations."

Patty beamed with pleasure and Sam's opinion of Murphy went up yet another notch when he served the little girl hot chocolate in a beer mug, complete with a frothy head of whipped cream.

"Is there really that much to say about fractions?" Murphy asked, scratching his head.

"Beats me," said Sam. "I stopped understanding most of what Patty has to say about seven years ago. If I didn't have the stretch marks, I'd think she was an alien visitor from some advanced planet."

"How do you keep up with her?"

"I don't." Sam took a sip of Murphy's rich dark coffee. "I feed her, clothe her and love her, but I sure as heck don't keep up with her."

Murphy looked toward Patty. "Some responsibility."

"Tremendous responsibility," said Sam, "but I can't imagine what my life would have been like without her. She's the best thing that's ever happened to me."

A series of expressions flickered across Murphy's face, and even Sam, who wasn't inclined toward analysis, saw both affection and admiration in his eyes.

"You're a lucky woman."

"Yes," she said, glancing toward her daughter. "I am, at that."

It was a tender, sweet moment. The kind of moment you wanted to stretch on and on. The kind of moment that futures were built on. Unfortunately, Patty and Scotty chose that moment to burst into peals of laughter that rattled the rafters of the bar.

"I never knew math was that funny," said Murphy.

"Neither did I." Sam raised her eyebrows in the direction of her daughter but Patty paid no heed. "I think they're up to something." *No matchmaking, kiddo, I'm warning you. Friendship is every bit as wonderful as romance.* And maybe if she repeated that phrase often enough, she might believe it....

Murphy grunted and poured himself a tall glass of club soda with a twist of lime. "He probably told her about Saturday night."

Sam's heart did a funny kind of thud against her breastbone. "Saturday night?" *Please don't tell me about the Playboy bunny/astrophysicist/humanitarian you're taking out to dinner.*

"The masquerade ball." He took a long gulp of club soda. "You're going, aren't you?"

Sam shook her head. "Not this year."

"Why not? You belong to the association. You're opening your store in a few weeks. You should be there along with everybody else."

"Tell that to my bank balance and my wardrobe."

"I was hoping to see you there."

Sure, you were. I could sit down and have a drink with you and your beautiful blue-eyed blond date.

"You'll have to settle for seeing me over my hors d'oeuvre trays tomorrow."

"Sounds good, but I won't be around tomorrow."

"Oh." *Don't sound so disappointed, Sam. What he does and where he does it aren't any of your business.*

"I'm going into Manhattan."

"I see."

"I have an appointment with UPI."

"An overseas assignment?"

"I'm hoping."

Sidewalk cafés. Elegant Frenchwomen with cheek-bones to die for. Moonlight walks near the Champs d'Elysé. "Good luck."

"I probably won't get the job. I'm still technically with the *Telegram*."

"I thought you quit the *Telegram*."

"Yeah, but there's a contract and they tend to get real touchy about things like that."

"I still think you'll get the job." Murphy O'Rourke didn't strike Sam as a man who lost out very often, not once he put his mind to something.

"You're an optimist."

"My biggest fault," said Sam. "I always believe people will get their fondest wishes."

"What about your fondest wishes?" He leaned closer; she could almost feel his intensity. "Will they come true?"

"I'm trying," said Sam, "but so far my fairy god-mother hasn't found me."

"Too bad you aren't going to the party. Maybe your fairy godmother will be there looking for you."

"Right," said Sam with a rueful laugh. "And maybe she'll turn me into Cinderella."

TWO TABLES AWAY, Patty and Professor Scotty exchanged knowing glances.

"Cinderella!" Patty breathed softly. "It's so romantic. I can't wait to see her face."

"And I can't wait to see his," said Scotty. "This is a fine plan, my dear child. A fine plan."

"I knew the minute I saw Murphy that he was the one."

"I wonder how long it will take them to agree with our assessment."

"My mom can be real stubborn."

"Murphy has been known to dig in his heels."

"My mom thinks Rocky Hill is the best place in the world."

"Murphy was looking for a way out from the day he was born."

"She thinks marriage is forever."

"He's been divorced."

They looked over at Sam and Murphy who were engaged in intense conversation, their heads pressed close together over the appetizer tray like old friends exchanging intimate confidences.

Patty grinned at the older man. "I think they're a match made in heaven."

He patted her hand. "So do I, dear girl. So do I."

Chapter Nine

It struck Murphy halfway through his interview with the chief honcho of UPI on Friday morning that he should be a hell of a lot happier.

So far everyone liked him, from the secretaries to the cub reporters to the executives who wouldn't know how to file a wire story if their collective lives depended on it. Every time he turned a corner he bumped into a familiar face and fielded another invitation to have lunch or dinner or drinks ASAP.

They were going to make an offer. Murphy didn't have a doubt in the world that they would. Interviews at his stage of the game were strictly *pro forma* matters. Social exercises rather than business deals. Sometime between now and Christmas the phone would ring and this seriously intelligent man on the other side of the desk would make an offer that would be just shy of knocking Murphy's socks off.

It was exactly what he'd thought he wanted back when he stormed out of the *Telegram* office in late October. Why then was he finding it so damned hard to muster up any enthusiasm?

You've had things your own way all your life. Why should this be any different?

Leave me alone, Pop.

Getting ready to run again, boy?

I only came back for you, Pop. I wanted to help.

Some help. How can I relax when I know you got one foot out the door?

I'm only thinking of you. Dr. Cohen says you should be doing more.

And what do you care, Mr. Big Shot? You've been too busy running all over Europe to care what happens in Rocky Hill.

That doesn't make any sense, Pop. First you tell me I want out, then you tell me I'm taking the bar away from you. Which is it?

"Murphy?"

Murphy jumped at the sound of his name. "Yes?"

The chief honcho laughed politely. "I asked if you want to go up to the dining room for lunch."

"Sure," said Murphy, rising from his chair. "I'm in no rush to get back."

"The Dover sole is superb."

Murphy smiled as the other man rose. "I'll consider it."

He knew it wouldn't hold a candle to the hearty, delicious concoctions Sam Dean had been supplying the past few days.

"It feels like the old days on the Geneva beat, doesn't it?" asked the chief honcho as they headed toward the private elevator at the end of the hall.

"Sure does," said Murphy, his tone bland.

"Those were the days," sighed the executive.

No, thought Murphy in surprise. As good as those days had been they couldn't hold a candle to the fun he'd had in the snow with Samantha Dean.

Don't even think it, boy. You're everything that woman and her kid don't need. You'd only hurt them when you left.

Shut up, Dad. This time you're probably right.

IT WASN'T THE SAME without Murphy.

Sam was amazed to discover how much she missed seeing him Friday afternoon when she stopped off at O'Rourke's to leave the trays of sandwiches and appetizers for the gang. Not even Scotty's courtly manners and effusive praise for her daughter's brilliance could ease the void Murphy's absence created.

Sam fumed all the way to Princeton Junction and her storefront. Scotty had said that O'Rourke would send a cousin around later to return the empty trays. What kind of nonsense was that anyway?

He's only being considerate, Sam. There's no reason to get all bent out of shape.

He had a life of his own. He had every right to spend the day in Manhattan job hunting, if that's what he wanted to do. What correspondent in his right mind wouldn't welcome a job offer from UPI? Just because her future was there in New Jersey was no reason to imagine the Garden State held any long-term allure for O'Rourke.

Her stint as chief cook for O'Rourke's Bar and Grill was as temporary as his stint as bartender. In fact, someone was interviewing for the spot that very afternoon. Soon his dad would be back mixing drinks and a cook would man the stove in the kitchen, and she and Murphy would go their separate ways.

In just a few days Murphy had become part of her daily life. She looked forward to seeing him, to talking to him, to making him laugh with stories about her years in cooking school and her tribulations raising a girl genius. He could be sardonic and he could be silly and while he wasn't the polished, sophisticated man of her dreams, he possessed a rough-and-tumble attractiveness that could be quite appealing.

The simple fact of the matter was she liked him. She liked him a lot. It was wonderful to be around a man who found the details of your everyday life as fascinating as Murphy seemed to find hers. She couldn't think of too many thirty-six-year-old men who would have been able to enjoy an impromptu snowball fight with the same zest that Murphy showed the night before.

"So where are you then, O'Rourke?" she said to the empty storefront. Why wasn't he back at the bar where he belonged, keeping Scotty and Joe and the rest of the gang company?

And, while she was asking questions he'd never answer, why was he taking another woman to the Tri-County Small Business Association's Annual Masquerade Ball?

WHEN SAM GOT HOME from working at the store, Patty and Caroline were seated at the kitchen table, chatting away like old ladies at a quilting bee, and Sam found herself annoyed that Patty hadn't seen fit to at least take something out of the freezer for dinner.

"Are you staying for dinner?" she snapped at her best friend.

Caroline's pale brows arched. "Such a gracious invitation, Samantha. It breaks my heart to decline."

Caroline stayed a few more minutes, and Sam managed to muster up enough enthusiasm to give the woman a quick hug good-bye.

"Are you okay?" Caroline asked before she disappeared down the driveway to her car. "You're not yourself."

"Don't I wish," Sam muttered, glaring at her beautiful blond blue-eyed friend.

"You're overtired." Caroline turned up the collar of her cashmere coat. "Get a good night's sleep. Everything will look brighter in the morning."

"Hah!" Sam shivered as a blast of cold air whipped around her shoulders. "A likely story."

"Trust me," said Caroline, winking at Patty. "I know what I'm talking about."

"What was that all about?" Sam asked the minute she closed and locked the door.

Patty's eyes were wide and innocent behind her glasses. "What was what?"

"That wink."

"What wink?"

"You and Caroline are up to something, aren't you?"

Patty looked away, her braids falling forward over her shoulders.

Sam sighed loudly and tugged at one of her daughter's plaits. "Don't encourage Caroline," she warned. "We made a pact not to exchange Christmas gifts this year and I, for one, intend to stick with it."

To Sam's horror, Patty's lower lip trembled. "I hate it when you say things like that."

Sam scrunched down next to her little girl. "You know our budget, sweetheart. I'd rather spend my money on—" She stopped, suddenly uncertain whether or not the Santa Claus issue had been satisfactorily resolved last year.

"That's all right," said Patty, her voice breaking. "I know Santa Claus is just a myth for children, and I know you want to get me presents but—" Her narrow shoulders shook as Sam gathered her into her arms.

"Don't cry, kiddo. I know I've done a lot of complaining about bills this year, what with the store and school and everything, but Christmas will be the same as it ever was. I promise you."

"I know," said Patty, her eyes glistening with tears. "That's the problem." She sniffled loudly. "I wish we could have the Christmas candles outside this year."

"The candles aren't free, honey. Besides, don't we have enough to do with decorating the *inside* of the house?" Their neighborhood had a long-standing Christmas tradition that Sam devoutly wished would disappear. Every Christmas Eve the residents lined their driveways and the street with tiny white paper bags. Inside each bag a fat white candle rested in a bed of sand. At dusk the candles were lighted and the flickering flames burned until well past midnight, ushering in Christmas with a festive—and Sam had to admit, lovely—way.

For years Patty had been begging Sam to let them join in the spectacle, but Sam had always been too broke to buy the supplies or too busy working until late on Christmas Eve to participate. And there was certainly no way on earth she would let her daughter, brilliant though she was, play with fire.

Sam knew she'd acquired the nickname "Mrs. Scrooge" from her family for her avid disinterest in all things Yule these past few years but she'd never imagined Patty had taken it so to heart.

"I don't think you're fair," Patty said, pouting.

"Just you wait until the store opens and we start to show a profit."

"I don't care about that."

"Sure you do, honey. Maybe we could even get you that computer you love so much."

"I don't care about some stupid computer." Patty pulled out of Sam's grasp. "I just want you to be happy!"

"I am happy, Patty." Where on earth had this come from? A second ago they'd been talking about the luminaria that lined the street on Christmas Eve.

"No, you're not."

"Of course I am! How could I be anything but happy with a daughter like you?"

"I won't be with you forever," said her brilliant, but painfully young, little girl. "One day I'll go off to college and you'll be all alone."

Out of the mouths of babes... Sam's heart twisted. It seemed as if Patty had been at the center of her life for as long as she could remember. She'd grown up just one step ahead of her baby daughter and found it impossible to imagine her life being any other way.

"Don't rush things, sweetheart. There's still plenty of time."

"I wish you were married," Patty blurted out. "I wish I had a father."

What point was there to reminding Patty that she did, indeed, have a father? Expensive presents at Christmas and birthdays did not a father make. Ronald Donovan was nothing more than a name on a birth certificate, tucked away in a safety deposit box and all but forgotten.

"You have Grandpa Harry and all of your uncles," Sam offered, removing Patty's glasses and drying them with the hem of her soft cotton sweater.

"But they don't belong to me."

"People don't belong to other people," Sam reasoned, although she knew all too well what her daughter meant. "There are an awful lot of people who love and care about you, Patty. That's not something to take lightly." She slipped the glasses back on her daughter's serious, freckled face.

Was that a twinkle she saw in her daughter's bright blue eyes? "I still wish I had a real dad living right here with us."

"I'm afraid you only have a real live mother and she'll have to be enough."

"I still wish you were married."

Sam laughed and shrugged her shoulders. "Well, sometimes, kiddo, so do I."

"Really?"

"Really." The years from seventeen to twenty-eight had disappeared in the blink of an eye. Sam felt as if she'd gone from schoolgirl to mother in an instant. Her life had been filled with caring for Patty's ever-increasing needs, earning a living, then the back-breaking job of school and starting a new business.

Even if she had been interested in romance along the way, she doubted if she'd have been able to squeeze a man into her schedule.

Funny how Murphy O'Rourke had been able to fit right into her schedule, making himself a part of her routine as if they'd been friends for years instead of only a few short days. She thoroughly enjoyed his company, and Patty was positively smitten in a way that Sam had never seen before.

Admit it, Sam—you're pretty smitten with him yourself.

She blushed under her daughter's knowing glance. Fat lot of good it did, being smitten with Murphy O'Rourke. He thought of her as a funny-looking younger sister and nothing more. She wasn't his type, and nothing on earth was going to change that.

Besides, if she were going to get serious about a man at last, she certainly wouldn't pick a footloose and fancy-free foreign correspondent as her heart's desire.

No, she wanted a quiet and stable businessman whose roots were as firmly entrenched in central New Jersey as hers were. She wanted a man whose idea of high excitement was running down to K-mart for a new snow shovel.

And, more than anything, she wanted a man who thought tall, skinny brunettes with brilliant red-haired daughters were the answer to a single man's dream.

Murphy O'Rourke?

Not very likely.

Sam sighed and kissed her daughter's cheek. "C'mon, kiddo. Give me a smile. We're in this together, just you and me."

"Yes," said Patty, forcing an answering smile. "Just you and me."

MURPHY HUNG OUT in Manhattan for a few hours after his meeting with the chief honcho at UPI. He wandered in and out of some of his old favorite watering holes, half hoping to bump into some of his pals from the *Telegram*, but no dice. Apparently other men his age had more important things to do.

In fact, they were probably all hot on the trail of a story that would have won Murphy the Pulitzer.

You made your bed, son, now you have to lie in it.

"Shut up, Pop, will you?"

"Say what?" The young, muscular parking attendant glared at Murphy through his mirrored lenses. "You got a problem, man?"

"No problem," said Murphy as another steroid-happy attendant brought his rented car to a squealing halt two inches away from Murphy's midsection. "Just another wonderful day in the Big Apple."

Traffic on Ninth Avenue was backed up halfway to Wall Street, and Murphy had to maneuver his way around a water main break, potholes and sidewalk Santas to get down to the Holland Tunnel and take an alternate route back to the sanity of central New Jersey.

As it was, he snarled his way home and stormed into the bar a little after six with all the charm of Conan the Barbarian.

"Down, boy!" One of the regulars hoisted a wooden chair and aimed its sturdy legs at Murphy who considered biting them off and spitting toothpicks at the clientele.

"I take it your meeting was unproductive?" Scotty's tone was smooth and conciliatory.

"Mmmph." Murphy's tone was not.

"Traffic heavy?"

"Hmmph." *Good going, O'Rourke.* Prehistoric man was probably a better conversationalist. He wanted to complain about the traffic, about the crowds in the city, about UPI and the demise of expense-account lunches but, to his surprise, there wasn't anybody in that bar he could talk to.

Scotty would lecture him on responsibility. His old man, who was watching him from behind the bar, would tune him out with a quick "I told you so." Angela, the waitress, would snort and tell him about her sore feet and varicose veins.

Sam would listen.

The thought was there, full-blown, as if it had been waiting in some dusty corner of his brain for him to notice. Sam was strong and opinionated, it was true, but there was a warmth about her that intrigued him. She was independent and ambitious and all of those terrific things but she was also a woman and that was what called to Murphy that night.

He tossed his tie and his trenchcoat over the bar and grabbed for his leather jacket hanging on the wall hook. "I'll be back in a few hours."

His father looked up from counting swizzle sticks. "Unfinished business?"

"Yeah," said Murphy, heading for the door. "Unfinished business."

AS IT TURNED OUT, Sam was harder to find than the Holy Grail. Her telephone number was unlisted. He couldn't remember if she lived in big Rocky Hill or little Rocky Hill and once he got that straight he called her Dane instead of Dean. Finally he called on one of his pals on the local police force to at least point him in the right direction. An hour and a half after his quest began, he turned onto a quiet street of middle-aged frame houses with neatly fenced yards. Number thirteen, nineteen—there it was. Twenty-three Harvest Drive.

The house with the police car in the driveway.

IT WAS DEFINITELY one of those days.

First Murphy wasn't at the bar. Then Patty lured her into one of those deep, soul-searching conversations about wanting a father that invariably tore at Sam's heartstrings and called up all manner of maternal guilt. Now her cousin Teddy, a twenty-year man on the local police force, decided to stop by and drop a bombshell on her doorstep.

"Frank's getting married this weekend!" Sam's voice rose an octave in surprise.

Teddy, a big bear of a man, laughed as he gulped down a cup of coffee in the front hall. "I can't believe it, either. Never thought he'd give me a sister-in-law, that's for darn sure."

Frank was Teddy's twin, equally big and equally jovial. Sam couldn't count the times both men had pitched in to help her and Patty over the rough spots. Frank operated a hot-dog cart in mid-Manhattan, which turned into that New York City perennial each Christmas—a roasted chestnut stand.

"So what's the deal, Teddy? Does he need the wedding catered?" The thought of turning out one hundred dinners on short notice made Sam blanch but there wasn't anything she wouldn't do for her cousin. She was already planning her shopping list.

"He's renting Uncle Joe's restaurant."

Sam whistled. "I'm impressed."

"What he needs is—" Teddy stopped and peered out the glass panel next to the door. "You expecting company?"

"No, I'm—oh, yeah. A delivery boy is coming by to return some trays."

"Pretty old delivery boy," said Teddy. "Looks kind of rough around the edges, if you ask me."

"Murphy!" Sam leaped to the door and swung it open, battling down a sudden rush of excitement racing through her veins. "What are you doing here?" *Brilliant, Sam! Talk about a gracious hostess...*

He waved the round metal trays overhead. "You need these, don't you?"

Teddy broke in with a theatrical cough. "You know this guy, Sammy?"

Her cheeks reddened as she ushered Murphy into her growing-smaller-by-the-second front hall. "Teddy, this is Murphy O'Rourke. His dad owns O'Rourke's Bar and Grill."

"Know it well," said Teddy, extending his paw of a hand. "Spent many a happy hour in there. How's your dad doing?"

Murphy's hazel eyes widened. "Great. He should be back behind the bar full-time in a few weeks."

"Glad to hear it. I know he had a rough spell of it there for a while."

"I love small towns," Murphy grumbled, just loud enough for Sam to hear. He looked at Teddy. "And you're—?"

"Sammy's cousin. Teddy Dean."

Teddy looked from Sam to Murphy then back again, and she didn't like what she saw in his eyes. In the best of times her family was both curious and talkative. Murphy's visit would be common knowledge from Rocky Hill to Trenton and back before Murphy finished his first cup of coffee. That was, if he had come to stay.

She cleared her throat. "Teddy dropped by to tell me my cousin Frank is getting married on Sunday."

Murphy nodded politely, obviously unenthralled by the Dean family saga.

"And you'll work the stand Sunday during the wedding?" Teddy said, forcing his full attention back to Sam.

"What stand?" asked Murphy.

"A chestnut stand." Sam laughed at the expression on his face. "You know—'Chestnuts roasting on an open fire...'"

"You're kidding."

"Hell, no!" said Teddy. "Frankie's got the best location in Manhattan. Right near Rockefeller Center. Makes a mint, too, let me tell you."

Sam thought of the many kindnesses both cousins had showed her over the years. "Of course, I will."

"You can keep the profits."

She waved away his words. "That's my wedding gift to them."

"He'll be back on Monday morning, bright and early."

Murphy snapped back to attention. "He only needs one day off?"

Teddy shrugged his huge, uniformed shoulders. "He's in love but he's not crazy. There's time for a honeymoon after the holidays. Too much money to be made in December."

"What a family," muttered Murphy, and Sam gave him a sharp jab in the ribs with her elbow. "Do you all sell food?"

"Just about," said Sam. "What else do you do when you love to eat as much as our clan does?"

Teddy looked down at his ample belly. "Only our Sammy here can eat and not pay the price."

"I'm lucky," said Sam. "Fast metabolism."

"I think she could use a few pounds," offered Murphy, dodging Sam's elbow.

"So do I," said Teddy.

"I think it's time to call it a night," said Sam with a glance at Murphy. "Don't you have crime to fight, Teddy?"

As if on cue, Teddy's squad car erupted in a series of squawks. "I think I'm being paged." He hesitated, once again looking from Murphy to Sam.

"Good-bye, Teddy," said Sam, opening the door wide.

Teddy winked at Murphy then chucked Sam under the chin. "Good night, you two."

Sam closed the door after her cousin then bolted the lock with a flourish. She leaned against the jamb and wiped imaginary perspiration from her brow. "Sorry you had to meet Teddy so early in our friendship. He's quite a character."

"That squad car gave me a scare," Murphy admitted as she led him into the kitchen. "I was afraid something had happened to you or Patty."

"Impossible," said Sam, switching off the television and putting up water for coffee. "Patty and I have too many guardian angels hovering over us."

Murphy straddled a chair, his gaze never leaving her. She caught her reflection in the door of her microwave oven. No wonder. She looked rotten. The ubiquitous ponytail. No makeup. Cheeks smeared with cake flour; vanilla extract instead of French perfume. And for sheer glamour, there was nothing like a faded blue chenille robe and sweat socks.

If she had a brain she'd take the cake out of the oven and stick her head in there instead.

"Excuse me, Murphy," she said, inching her way toward the door. "I'm going to change my clothes."

"Why?" He looked genuinely confused. "You look fine to me."

Of course you do, Sam. He's looking for a cup of coffee, not a romantic encounter.

She turned back to the counter and fussed with coffee beans and filters as if kitchen chores were foreign to her. At that moment, everything felt foreign—the fit of her skin, her thoughts, the odd sensation of having a man like Murphy in her country kitchen on a cold winter's night. "How was your day in the big city?"

"Okay."

She caught the hesitation in his voice and turned around to meet his eyes. "That bad?"

He nodded. "That bad."

"I'm a good listener." The aroma of freshly brewed coffee filled the air, mingling with the smell of cinnamon and cloves.

He reached for her hand and drew her closer. "I need one tonight, Sam."

Her heart thundered wildly inside her chest. "Well, I'm here."

"I'm glad."

"So am I," said Sam. "Now tell me all about your day."

And, while you're at it, tell me who you're taking to the Masquerade Ball . . .

STRANGE.

Murphy was only halfway into the story of his rotten day in the Big Apple when it happened. His anger, his fatigue, the general sense of going nowhere fast vanished completely. He finished his story, camping it up to make Sam laugh, but the rage that had driven it was long gone.

She had a great laugh, Sam Dean had, full-bodied and unself-conscious, tinged with the innocence of childhood but all woman. Definitely all woman. He couldn't remember the last time he'd just sat in a real-life kitchen and talked with a woman who listened. Really listened. Sam was warm and attentive and not shy about telling him when he was acting like a horse's hind quarter—which apparently was a hell of a lot.

"More coffee?" He watched as she walked over to the refrigerator for the pitcher of milk. Amazing how many curves she had hidden beneath that shapeless robe. A clear picture of the way she'd looked running across the parking lot that first morning at the bar passed before his eyes and he grinned. Long slender legs leading into gently rounded hips with a waist he could span with his hands and—

She was looking at him curiously. "Was that a no, Murphy?"

"No—I mean, yes." What it was, was a groan. He had no business thinking about Sam like that. "I should be hitting the road. This is the bar's busiest time."

She didn't disagree, and he suddenly felt awkward and clumsy, as if he'd overstayed his welcome.

He followed her into the hall—doing his best not to imagine the way she looked beneath her robe—mumbling all sorts of apologies for barging in on her.

She tossed him his coat, her lovely face lit with laughter. "Good grief, O'Rourke! I can't stand it when you're humble."

"You probably had plans for tonight."

She looked down at her attire. "Right. I was going to sew up a gown for the Masquerade Ball."

"You're going?" Maybe wasting a Saturday night with a bunch of stuffed shirts would have a compensation.

"Afraid not."

"Any chance you'll change your mind?"

"On, maybe one in seven million."

"I'll be banking on it, Sam." *Stupid, sappy line, O'Rourke. Since when do you spout mush like that? This is Sam you're talking to, not some air-headed bimbo from the Upper West Side.*

"Have fun tomorrow," she said, tossing her ponytail back over her shoulder. Did she have any idea how graceful such a simple gesture could seem?

"I'd say I have a one-in-seven-million chance of that."

"Congratulate Scotty on his award."

He nodded. Her dark brown gaze moved from his chin to his mouth and back to meet his eyes. Her tongue darted out to moisten her lower lip and he had the urge to pull her up close to him and kiss her thoroughly.

Ridiculous! She'd probably laugh in his face and tell him he'd been out of circulation too long.

Which, all things considered, was probably right.

"See you Monday?" he asked, turning up the collar on his jacket and stepping out onto the cold front step.

"See you Monday," said Sam.

Head down against the wind, he ran toward his car and made his way back to the bar.

"You okay?" asked his father when Murphy took over.

"Fine," said Murphy.

"You figure out whatever was eating at you?"

"No," he said, "but somehow it doesn't matter anymore."

His problems were still there waiting to be solved, but for one evening Sam had made it all seem very far away.

Chapter Ten

"Mom."

Sam groaned and pressed her face deeper into her pillow. "Go away," she mumbled. "It's not even dawn yet."

"Mom, wake up."

"Have a heart, Patty. At least let me sleep until the sun comes up."

"Get up, you lazy wretch!" There was only one woman on earth with the sugar-coated voice of a martinet. "It's almost ten."

"Go home, Caroline. Go bother someone else."

"We're going to have to resort to drastic measures," she heard Caroline say through her still-sleepy brain.

I'm dreaming all of this, she thought, drifting back toward sleep. *This isn't really happening.*

"Maa-a-a!" Patty's voice was high with anxiety. "You absolutely must wake up this minute!"

"No," said Sam, squeezing her eyes closed as tight as possible. She was in the middle of the most delightful dream about Murphy and their unexpected time together last night, and she wanted it to go on and on . . . "I am not waking up. Not for anybody."

"But you're a mother." Patty sounded scandalized and Sam smiled.

"No, I'm not. I hereby resign the position until a decent hour."

"Sorry, kid." Sam felt a hand grip the edge of the blankets. "I didn't want to play rough with you but—"

With that, the hand executed a perfect snap of the wrist that sent the bedclothes flying to the floor, and Sam sat straight up, gasping in the cool morning air in the bedroom, as Patty and Caroline looked on, amused.

"This is barbaric." She grabbed for the blankets but Caroline kicked them out of reach.

"Rise and shine," said her best friend.

"It must be six in the morning."

"Nine on the dot," said Patty with a smug smile.

Sam fell back against the pillows and covered her eyes with her hand. "I need caffeine."

"At your service." Caroline stepped out of the room, then returned with a white wicker tray heaped with serving dishes. "Caffeine, carbohydrates and an egg."

Sam uncovered her eyes and leaned up on her elbows.

Patty scrambled across the mattress and sat by Sam's uncovered, icy-cold knees. "Merry Christmas from Aunt Caroline."

Caroline placed the breakfast tray over Sam's narrow hips and removed the lid on the platter of perfectly toasted blueberry muffins. "Say one word about not exchanging presents, Samantha, and you'll be wearing the eggs."

"But we promised!" Sam felt awash in pleasure, embarrassment and a touch of righteous dismay. "No presents until our businesses are in the black."

"Mine's been in the black for two years now, kiddo, and I refuse to wait any longer."

If only the muffins didn't smell so incredibly delicious. "I said only Patty gets presents this year."

"Oh, stop being so tedious, Ms Scrooge, and eat your damned breakfast!"

Patty giggled as Caroline sat down in the slipper chair near the window.

Sam uncovered the fluffy yellow eggs and lifted the lid on the china pot of English breakfast tea. "I do hate to waste food."

Patty poured the dark tea into Sam's cup and liberally sugared it. Sam didn't have the heart to tell her daughter that she hadn't used sugar in her tea for at least eight years.

"Aunt Caroline has a whole day planned for you."

Sam almost choked on her sip of tea as she turned to face her best friend. "What is Patty talking about?"

Caroline leaned back and stretched her legs out in front of her. "Luxury, Samantha. Pure, unadulterated luxury."

The sweet, fruity smell of the blueberry muffins proved to be too much for Sam and she bit into one greedily. The plump, warm berries burst with flavor inside her mouth. "I can deal with breakfast in bed," she said, with a sheepish smile.

Patty's small frame relaxed beside her, and her daughter cadged a piece of the second muffin. "There's more, Mom." Patty turned toward Caroline, who still looked as if she hadn't a care in the world.

"This is your day, Sam. Today your secret wishes will all come true."

Sam's cheeks reddened as she remembered one of more interesting dreams about Murphy. "You painted the store for me?"

"Something more personal than that."

"You paid my phone bill."

Caroline waved her manicured hand in the air. "Don't be ridiculous. That's small potatoes."

A tiny thrill blossomed way down deep, in a part of Sam's heart that hadn't seen daylight in a very long time. "The masquerade ball tonight?"

"The masquerade ball," said Caroline.

Sam's heart was thudding so wildly she could scarcely think. "I can't," she whispered. "My hair... my nails... I don't have a thing to—" *Murphy's going to be there!*

"Yes, you do." Caroline rose from the chair and disappeared into the hallway.

Sam grabbed Patty's hand to keep from spinning away in pure excitement as she heard Caroline's footsteps returning.

"Voilà!" Caroline called from just outside the bedroom door. "Instant glamour, at your service!"

"Oh, my God!" Sam's eyes swam with tears as she stared at the glorious sapphire-blue satin confection draped across Caroline's arms. "Old Frosty's gown!"

"Yours for the night, Cinderella!"

"But, look at me." Sam stared down at her work-roughened hands, her unpainted nails, the reflection of her unmadeup face in the mirror across the room. "I'm a disaster."

"After I'm through with you, you won't be."

"Please, Mom!" Patty gave her an awkward hug around the breakfast tray. "Please go to the ball tonight!"

Think of it, Sam! You've worked so hard for so long—what could possibly be wrong with having one night to really shine?

"There's so little time. I still have the food trays to make for O'Rourke's and—"

"Everything's been taken care of," Caroline broke in. "All you have to worry about is being beautiful."

"And I suppose you're my fairy godmother?"

"Yes. That's exactly who I am tonight."

Forget it, her mind warned. *He has a date.* It didn't matter what magic Caroline wrought, for even the strongest alchemy couldn't turn her into a cuddly blue-eyed blonde.

But her woman's heart was sending out some strong messages of its own. *Go! Smile and dance and have a wonderful time. Let him see you at your best, even if only to show him what he missed.*

"I'll do it," she said, laughter bubbling through her apprehensions. "I'll go to the ball!"

Even if it meant watching Murphy O'Rourke having the time of his life with the type of woman Sam could never be.

PATTY THOUGHT her heart would burst through her chest as she looked at her beautiful mother glide into the room ten hours later, with Aunt Caroline fussing at her heels. There wasn't a model or movie star anywhere in the entire world who could possibly look as glorious as her mom did that very moment!

"Well?" Sam stopped before Patty and looked down at her. "What do you think, kiddo?"

"Wow!" Patty managed over the great big lump in her throat. "You look...oh, wow!"

"I think we're a success," her mom said to Caroline with a nervous laugh.

"You're beautiful," said Caroline who looked wonderful in a slinky beaded black dress that seemed to stay up through sheer willpower alone. "You look like a princess in a fairy tale."

"You're Cinderella," Patty said, touching the shimmering sapphire folds of the full satin skirt.

"Well, I'm certain I won't find Prince Charming at the Tri-County Masquerade Ball." Sam tilted her head slightly and Patty caught the delicate tinkle of her rhinestone drop earrings as her mother looked into the standing mirror Caroline had brought over. "I don't think I'd recognize myself in a crowd." She held the sequined and feathered white velvet mask up to her face. "A woman of mystery! Who would have believed it possible?"

"I would," said Caroline, smoothing Sam's Gibson Girl upsweep with one gloved hand. "I always knew the potential was there, didn't you, Patty?"

Patty nodded vigorously. She knew her mom was pretty, if disinterested in her looks, but never in a million years had she imagined that under Sam's baggy cords and shapeless sweaters and straggly ponytail hid movie star material! Maybe growing up had some advantages besides being able to start work on a Ph.D. Could Patty possibly have such a wonderful surprise in store for her in another fifteen years?

"Wow!" she said again. She would have to remember to apologize to her friend Susan. Apparently there were times when no other word would suffice.

"Well, well!" Grandma Betty came from the kitchen, wiping her hands on her apron. "I never thought I'd see the day!"

"Neither did I," said Sam as she pirouetted gracefully.

Patty sighed as the full skirt of the satin gown made wonderful swishy noises with each movement.

"You're beautiful, Samantha," said Grandma Betty, who would watch Patty until the baby-sitter showed up.

Sam's eyes sparkled like the rhinestones twinkling at her ears. "I *feel* beautiful," she said in a voice as soft as her shiny dark hair.

The doorbell chimed and everybody jumped in surprise. Patty leaped up to answer it, swinging the front door open wide.

"If the ladies are ready, their car awaits," said a tall gray-haired man in a chauffeur's uniform complete with cap.

"Come on, Cinderella," said Caroline as she draped a wrap about Sam's shoulders. "The coach has arrived."

Sam bent down in front of Patty, who was sniffling and smiling and feeling an awful lot like a very little girl in front of her oh-so-glamorous mother.

"You'll be good for your grandmother, won't you?"

Patty nodded, not trusting her voice. She was so happy, and so hopeful, that she thought she could just spin out into orbit under her own power.

Sam kissed her lightly on the forehead and Patty almost swooned. Instead of smelling like cinnamon and sweet cream, her mom smelled like Shalimar. Her everyday mother was now exactly the kind of woman Patty imagined a man would love.

She looked over at her Aunt Caroline who flashed her a thumbs up sign. Patty waved good-bye from the front door. A full moon splashed across the snowy street. Winter stars twinkled high in the sky while Christmas carols seemed to blossom all around. Had there ever been an evening so absolutely *perfect* for romance?

The limousine eased silently down the driveway and headed up the street toward her mom's destiny. Unless she missed her guess, her mom and Murphy O'Rourke didn't stand a chance tonight, which was one hundred percent okay with Patty because she knew way down deep in her heart that this was the answer to all of her dreams.

She ran for the telephone and dialed Susan's number.

"Hello?"

"Susan, it's Patty."

Her friend squealed with excitement. "Did they go? How did your mom look? Has he seen her yet? Did you get a ride in the limousine? Did it have a bar and a television and—"

"Susan?"

"Yes?"

"Wow!"

MURPHY GAVE a final tug to his bow tie, straightened his cummerbund, then headed downstairs to meet up with Scotty.

"Wooo-eee!" Joe and Frank whistled and applauded as Murphy made his entrance. "Will you look at Beau Brummel there?"

Murphy didn't dare look over at his dad who was tending bar tonight. Bill's rumbling laugh was enough.

"One word out of any of you bozos and you're history," Murphy growled as Scotty stepped forward. He turned to look at his educated pal. "And if you give me a corsage, I swear I'll—"

"A corsage?" Scotty's elegant brows lifted. "I had thought more along the lines of a simple nosegay to complement your eyes."

"I've been wondering who you're dating, Murph," called out one of the regulars from across the bar. "Robbing the rest home again, are you?"

His dad's deep laugh grew louder. "At least now I know why I don't have grandchildren from this one."

"I'm glad you jokers are having a great time at my expense."

"Philistines, all of them," said Scotty as he slipped into his topcoat.

Murphy grabbed for his own coat. "I'm getting the hell out of here," he mumbled, then made a beeline for the door with Scotty close behind.

It was only seven-thirty and already it was the worst night of Murphy's life.

THE LIGHTS WERE LOW. The music was grand and lush. Chandeliers twinkled like diamonds overhead; diamonds glittered like—well, like diamonds on the fingers of Princeton's old guard. The women were lavishly coiffed and expensively dressed while the men were suave and sophisticated in tuxedos and old-fashioned tails.

And, miracle of miracles, Sam fit right in. No, she more than fit in, she looked as if she belonged. The moment she stepped inside the grand ballroom she knew she was home free. Caroline's date had spotted the glamorous blonde immediately—even with the plumed and sequined mask in place—and before Caroline was spirited off into the crowd, she whispered "Break a leg!" and Sam was on her own.

She straightened her shoulders and held her head high. There was something to be said for dressing for success. She felt positively regal in this princess dress. The voluminous skirt rustled and the toes of her peau de soie pumps alternately appeared and disappeared with each step she took. Her shoulders were bare; the low neckline revealed a rather amazing amount of bosom for a woman used to wearing Arnold Schwarzenegger's cast-off sweaters.

How wonderful it felt to be the center of attention as she swept through the ballroom, a study in sapphire satin and nonchalance. Men watched her as she passed, their eyes glittering behind their black masks. Sam couldn't remember the last time she'd been the recipient of so many long and lingering looks. In fact, she was fairly certain she'd *never* been the recipient of so many long and lingering looks.

Unfortunately none of those looks belonged to Murphy O'Rourke.

Sam peered through her mask at each man she passed. Tall men. Short men. Fat men. Men with mustaches and beards and foreign accents. Either these masks were infinitely more concealing than she'd originally believed or Murphy was nowhere to be found. She scanned the room for beautiful blondes, assuming one of them was Murphy's date. Still no sign of him.

She accepted a flute of champagne from a waiter and declined an invitation to dance tendered by a tall, slender man with piercing dark eyes. *Where are you, O'Rourke?* she thought as she made her way across the room toward the French doors. *If I live to be one hundred, I'll never look this good again.*

The bubbles tickled her nose as she sipped her champagne. *All dressed up and no place to go.* The least he could do was put in an appearance so she could dazzle him! This was all Caroline's fault. Sam was about to search out her best friend and attach herself to Caroline's side like a burr when she heard a familiar voice.

"Good evening, Samantha. May I say you look especially lovely tonight?"

She spun around. "Scotty! It's so nice to see a friendly face."

The man pressed a kiss to her cheek. "I want you to meet my date."

Sam laughed. "Date! You've been keeping secrets." The older man took her arm and propelled her across the dance floor in the direction of the orchestra. "Who is she?"

"You're jumping to conclusions, Samantha," said Scotty in a cryptic fashion.

Her eyes widened behind her mask as they approached a man of medium height whose back was to them. Her cheeks flamed with embarrassment. "Oh, Scotty! I'm sorry...I mean I didn't...I never suspected that you were—"

The man spun around. It was Murphy O'Rourke.

Chapter Eleven

What on earth had happened to the rumpled, sloppy Murphy O'Rourke she thought she knew?

His sandy hair was beautifully barbered. His five-o'clock shadow was a thing of the past. His tux was tailored to fit his broad-shouldered frame and his shirtfront was snowy white and starched to perfection. Even his bow tie was exactly the way it should be.

"Murphy?" Her voice was wispy for it was hard to draw a breath. Her heart was beating so rapidly that she felt her pulse pounding in her ears, at the base of her throat, her wrists...

"Sam." She watched, enchanted, as the sparkle in his hazel eyes turned to something darker, more intense. "You're beautiful."

She ducked her head for a moment then remembered that this was a night for magic. "So are you."

"I thought you weren't coming tonight."

"I wasn't." She told him briefly about Caroline's surprise Christmas present. His eyes never left hers. A warm, tingly feeling blossomed inside her heart. "So here I am, the brand new, hundred percent improved version of Samantha Dean."

"I liked the old version, too," he said, taking her elbow and leading her toward the dance floor. "You looked pretty cute last night in your ponytail."

Sam's ponytail was now a thing of the past. She'd left it behind on the floor of the Shady Lady Hair Salon that afternoon. "I hope you didn't get rid of your corduroy jacket," she said as he took her champagne glass and deposited it on a side table. "I'm rather fond of it."

"This isn't me," said Murphy, gesturing toward his fancy clothes.

"And this isn't me, either," said Sam, motioning toward her glamorous garb. This was a fairy tale come true, complete with Cinderella and the handsome prince. She glanced down at her shoes, half expecting to see they had been transformed into glass slippers.

The lush sounds of romantic music from the Big Band era drifted over to where they stood. Sam longed to ask Murphy to dance but she couldn't summon up the nerve. How foolish! This was the same man she'd tumbled with in the snow just a few days earlier. The same man who had fallen across her legs and rubbed her face in the snow and kissed her on the cheek like a brother would kiss his kid sister. The same man who had sat at her kitchen table last night and made her laugh. She looked at him in his elegant clothes and wicked mask. Nothing had changed.

Yet everything had.

She knew it and, she suspected, so did he.

The music grew more poignant, more enticing.

Murphy cleared his throat. "Scotty's a matchmaker."

Sam swallowed hard. "So is Caroline."

His hazel eyes twinkled behind the mask. "Do you think we've been set up?"

"Oh, yes," said Sam, "and I think I know who's behind it all."

"Patty?"

She nodded. "Patty."

He took her hand then and drew her into his arms. "Remind me to thank the kid."

"Oh, I will." A deep sigh of pleasure rose up inside Sam as she went to him. His arms were strong as he held her close to his broad chest. He moved gently at first, his body barely swaying to the rhythm of the music, and it seemed to Sam—practical, down-to-earth Sam!—as if she'd been waiting all her life for this moment. The cut of the gown bared her back almost to the waist and a thrill of excitement shot through her as he rested his warm palm flat against the ridge of her spine. Her dangerously high heels made Sam closer to his height, and her temple brushed the strong curve of his jaw.

If only the orchestra would never stop playing....

THE FRENCH had a word for it, but then, the French had a word for all things romantic.

Coup de foudre. The lightning bolt.

The way Murphy had felt when he turned and looked at Samantha in that shimmering blue dress. The sight of her, tall and slender in that incredible gown, knocked the breath out of his lungs. For a long moment he couldn't think or speak or do anything but stare at her. Her arms and legs were long and finely made; her torso, gently curved. She held her head high; her slender throat was white and supple, encircled with a glittering necklace.

This was Sam. His friend Sam. The Sam who made sandwiches for the gang at the bar and laughed when he buried her face in a snowdrift. The same Sam who was mother and daughter and friend.

A few hours ago he would have sworn on a stack of Gideon bibles that their friendship would never be anything more than exactly that. Now, with her in his arms, he wondered how he could ever have been such a fool. The feelings that had thrown him for a loop last night in her kitchen hadn't been his imagination, after all. Whatever it was that made Sam *Sam*, had the power to mesmerize him whether she was dressed in a bathrobe or a satin gown. She was the most fascinating woman he'd ever met.

And the most desirable. Her skin was silk beneath his fingertips. Her hair held the scent of an exotic garden on a summer's day. The way her body fit against his made him rethink his position on Fate. She was an exotic stranger in his arms, and yet she was the same woman he'd come to know and care for this past week.

Murphy had waited thirty-six years and five months for a woman to sweep him off his feet and now that he'd found her, he wasn't about to let her go.

"LOOK AT THEM," said Caroline to Scotty as the happy couple danced past them. "They couldn't be more perfect together!"

"We should be quite proud of ourselves," said the professor.

"That we should."

Sam looked up at Murphy as if he were the sun and the stars. He looked down at Sam as if she held the keys to paradise. They glowed with delight and the newfound blush of discovery, and if Caroline wasn't so crazy about Sam she might have been envious.

"Murphy has always claimed he was not the marrying kind," said Scotty.

"Sam said she hasn't time for anything but Patty and her store."

She met Scotty's eyes and the two of them burst into delighted laughter.

"Shall we dance, my dear?"

"Charmed, Professor," said Caroline. They both knew it was only a matter of time.

"WE'VE BEEN DANCING for almost two hours," Murphy murmured against Sam's ear.

"I know," she whispered. "Isn't it wonderful?"

His grip tightened as he drew her yet closer to him. Her body went softer and more yielding, if that was possible. At that moment all things seemed possible. Boundaries and rules and her old ways of thinking no longer mattered. The shell around her heart had broken at last and she felt almost giddy with joy.

She was Sam and yet she wasn't. He was Murphy—and yet he was someone better, someone exciting and dangerous and potently masculine.

This couldn't be happening, and yet it was.

She sighed and rested her forehead against his shoulder.

Oh, it definitely was happening...

For the past week, Sam had thought of Murphy O'Rourke as a reporter, a bartender, a dirty snowball

fighter, and a brand new friend. The one way she tried
not to think of Murphy was as a man.

She knew he had problems with his dad and his
brother, that a lot of people wanted to hire him to report the news, and that there was a soft spot in his
heart for kids and damsels in distress. She also knew
there was an ex-wife somewhere out there in the world
and probably a good number of ex-girlfriends, as well,
but none of it had made a lasting impression upon her.

Oh, sure, she'd felt a prickle of envy when she
thought he'd be attending this party with some nubile
young blonde but the moment she saw him with the
not-so-nubile Scotty in tow, her envy vanished.

So did everything else, save for the overwhelming
sense that she was exactly where she should be, and at
the exact moment of time she should be there.

Don't get carried away, Sam, her internal censor
warned. *This isn't any more real than that dress you're
wearing or the* faux *diamonds around your neck.*
Come midnight Cinderella would have to leave the ball
and go home alone without Prince Charming because
that was the way life really was.

Murphy's arms tightened pleasurably about her. He
smelled faintly soapy, faintly spicy, altogether masculine and intoxicating. His body was warm and broad
and wonderfully powerful and he had an athletic grace
that translated beautifully to the dance floor. If her
fairy godmother appeared before her and said this
moment could go on forever, Sam would have pledged
her undying gratitude.

She floated through the evening on a cloud of excitement. Caroline joined them at the front of the
ballroom and they all applauded madly as the emi-

nent Professor Edmund MacTavish received his award. Scotty was such a splendid fellow! Caroline was such a wonderful friend!

She looked at the handsome, debonair Murphy O'Rourke and practically melted right there on the spot. And to think she owed it all to her precocious daughter. Sam was awash with tenderness, with excitement, with gratitude and happiness and—could it be?—a sudden, inexplicable rush of Christmas spirit. Why, she even found herself joining in with the crowd as they sang a lively version of "Deck the Halls."

Scotty rejoined them and she, Murphy, and Caroline toasted the older man's health and happiness. The orchestra started up once again and Sam went into Murphy's arms as naturally as drawing a breath. Not that drawing a breath was an easy task, for his closeness was having the most decidedly powerful effect upon the once staid and practical Samantha Dean.

"It's getting warm in here," said Murphy, his eyes sparkling behind the mask that tradition decreed should remain in place until the midnight hour.

She fanned herself delicately. "It certainly is."

He inclined his head toward the French doors across the ballroom. "Maybe we need some fresh air."

She nodded. "I think we do."

He danced her across the room in the blink of an eye, and before anyone could notice they slipped out onto the patio.

"Are you cold?" he asked.

"I should be but I'm not."

"It's almost time for the late-night supper." He traced the line of her jaw with the tip of his index finger. "Are you hungry?"

Sam shook her head. Let the others swarm into the dining room. She felt sorry for them. What was food compared with a moonlit winter night?

Tiny white lights glittered from the bare branches of the trees beyond the patio. From somewhere far away came the sounds of laughter and music and crystal glasses raised in a toast.

"I know it's not midnight," said Murphy, "but I think it's time to unmask."

She watched, spellbound, as he reached for his mask and slowly removed it. She'd thought herself on familiar terms with the planes and angles of his broad and masculine face but she felt as if she were seeing him for the very first time: those high strong cheekbones; the powerful jawline and stubborn chin; the fleeting dimples and off-center smile; those thick sandy lashes framing his hazel eyes. Why hadn't she noticed what a beautiful man he truly was?

She lifted her hand to remove her own mask.

"No." His voice was deep, commanding.

Taking a step toward her, he brought his large hands to her face and slowly removed her sequined velvet mask. Sam felt as if she were losing the last of her defenses against him.

"Hi, Sam," he said in a dark and dangerous voice she hadn't heard before.

Her hands trembled and she found it impossible to speak. The world seemed far away, as if they were suspended somewhere in infinite time.

Murphy reached forward and brushed a curl away from Sam's eyes. Such a gentle touch from such a strong and powerful man. That gentle touch was Sam's undoing. She lifted her eyes to meet his. He lowered his head toward her. Sam's lips parted; her pulses quickened.

This is it, she thought wildly. This was the moment they'd been moving toward all evening, the moment she'd been waiting for....

"Excuse us."

They leaped apart. A middle-aged couple, looking delightfully guilty, emerged from the shadows. "Sorry," said the woman with a giggle. "Don't want to miss dinner."

The man did his best to look dignified but the smudges of crimson lipstick near his mouth undid his valiant attempts.

Murphy's stormy expression matched her wildly churning emotions. "The roads are clear," he said, his voice almost a growl. "We could take a drive."

"Patty," Sam whispered. "Her sitter goes home at twelve-thirty."

He glanced at his watch. "An hour and a half," he said, slipping out of his tux jacket and draping it across her shoulders. "I'll have you back on time."

She smiled up at him, feeling coddled and cosseted and almost lethally feminine. "I'd love a moonlight drive."

If either had feared that the intrusion of reality would tarnish the lustre of the evening, their fears were groundless, for once they were tucked into the velvet darkness of the rented car, away from the sharp winter wind and prying eyes, the world dropped away once again.

"Where are we going?" Sam asked as he eased the car out of the parking lot.

"Someplace quiet."

A frisson of nervousness made Sam's breath catch for an instant. It was so dark and they were so alone. He drove slowly along Route 206, past stores and old houses and huge wooded areas yet to catch the land developer's eye. Turning right on tiny Highway 518, he headed up the winding curves toward Rocky Hill. Christmas candles burned in living room windows and colored lights twinkled around doorways. There were huge candy canes and wreathes with big shiny red bows. She could almost swear she heard the lilting voices of carolers in the distance. Sam smiled in the darkness of the car. What a wonderful season.

She cast him a quick glance. *What a wonderful man . . .*

Murphy made a right, then a left, and suddenly Sam knew exactly where they were headed. Five minutes later he pulled alongside the bridge that overlooked one of the Delaware-Raritan valley canals.

"I forgot you grew up around here," Sam said as he helped her from the car.

"This has always been one of my favorite spots." He put his arms around her shoulders and led her toward the railing. "Even when I wanted nothing more than to get the hell out of New Jersey, I still loved it here."

"You know what they call it, don't you?" The wind whipped up from the icy water but for some strange reason she didn't feel a thing.

He grinned at her. "Make-out Point."

"You knew."

"I know a lot of things, Sam."

"I'm sure you do," she said, her words tossed back at them by the wind. "You *are* an ace reporter."

He drew her into the circle of his arms as he had when they danced. "I know something special is happening."

She caught the scent of his skin, and warmth spread through her limbs. "You're going to kiss me, aren't you?"

He ducked his head lower to look at her. "That's the general idea."

He was so close she could see the shadow of his beard beneath his ruddy skin, imagine the feel of his mouth against hers, the way he would—

"I think this would be a good time," she said, her gaze resting on his lips.

"So do I." His head dipped toward her and an instant later his lips found hers. At first the pressure was light, almost teasing, and she found herself intrigued by the combination of steel and velvet his kiss called to mind.

Time curled around them as the seconds passed and with each one, Sam found herself drawing closer to him, yearning for a deeper, more intimate contact. Desire was a silken cord, binding her to him in exquisite anticipation.

It was as if he read minds, for suddenly his lips parted and she gasped as his tongue teased the place where her own lips met, then gained entry to her mouth. The champagne had left behind a fruity taste that mingled with a flavor reminiscent of brandy that was Murphy's own.

"So, here we are," Murphy said when he finally broke the kiss.

"Here we are," said Sam, drawing his face toward hers for another kiss.

Moonlight spilled over them, adding to the magical feeling that had followed them all evening. The way the snow sparkled, the silvery sheen of the water passing beneath the bridge, the eerie and beautiful designs the icy branches of the bare trees made against the night sky—all of it became part of Sam as she stood there cradled in Murphy's arms.

"I wasn't planning on this," said Murphy.

"Neither was I."

"That doesn't seem to matter much anymore, does it?"

"Not a bit."

"We don't have a lot in common."

"No, we don't."

"That doesn't matter either, does it?"

She sighed with pleasure. "I'm afraid not."

"So now what do we do?"

"I was hoping you'd have a few ideas."

"I do." He kissed her cheek, her nose, her forehead, moving slowly, tantalizingly, toward her mouth. "Open for me, Sam."

A long, voluptuous shiver rose up from the tips of her sparkly high heels to the top of her head. She was pure flame, a wildly erotic mass of nerve endings sensitized beyond endurance as she parted her lips and drew him into her mouth. She slid her hands up his chest and over his shoulders, feeling his heat burning through the fabric of his shirt. Burning through her body as his fingers gripped her waist under his jacket that was draped over her shoulder, then spanned her ribcage, easing upward inch by fiery inch toward the satin-covered curve of her breasts. He broke their kiss. Lowering his head, he pressed his lips against the hollow of her throat as a low moan began to build inside her.

Sensations that had been new and wonderful when she was sixteen were even more miraculous now that she was old enough to know the fragility of a moment like this. There were times in life when the better part of valor was to give over to emotion.

He bent his head toward her. She lifted her eyes to his. Their lips met again and—

"Anything wrong, folks?" Sam and Murphy leaped apart as the bright beam of a flashlight found them. "Kind of cold to be standing outside."

Sam squinted into the light and saw a familiar face at the other end of the flashlight. "Teddy? Is that you?"

The beam lowered. "Sam? What the hell are you doing out here?" He aimed the light directly at poor Murphy. "Hey, O'Rourke. Glad to see you."

Sam didn't dare wait for Murphy to respond.

"We were on our way back now," she said, certain she would be forgiven this small white lie. "Patty's sitter wants to go home by twelve-thirty."

Teddy checked his watch. "Better motor then, guys. Times a-wastin'. Besides, you'll need your sleep for tomorrow."

Sam's mouth dropped open. "Oh, my God! The chestnut stand."

"Don't tell me you forgot."

"Almost," said Sam.

"Then it's a good thing I bumped into you, isn't it?"

"Definitely an act of Fate," said Murphy, his expression deadpan.

"I think it's time to call it a night," said Sam, with a glance in Murphy's direction. "I have a busy day ahead of me tomorrow."

"What time do we get started?" asked Murphy.

We?

"Frank will have the stand set up by 10.00 a.m.," said Teddy as if he and O'Rourke had been lifelong cronies.

"You're coming with me?" asked Sam.

"Seems like that's the only way I'm going to see you tomorrow, doesn't it?"

She nodded, struck dumb with surprise. He really was a most remarkable man.

"We'll bring Patty," he continued as Teddy walked them to their car. "She'd probably get a kick out of the store windows and the tree. I've been promising to take my sister's boy in this season."

"Great idea," said Teddy, clapping Murphy on the back. "Use Frank's parking spot near Radio City. I'll make sure he okays it for you."

The two men shook hands. "Do I have anything to say about this?" Sam asked.

"Not a hell of a lot," said Murphy, putting his arm around her right there in front of her cousin Teddy, the town crier. Poor Murphy. Little did he know that was practically a declaration of intent in the Dean family. "If that's what I have to do to see you tomorrow, that's what I have to do."

"Looks like I'm leaving you in good hands, Sammy. I'll call Frank and tell him his wedding's on for tomorrow."

Teddy made to leave then turned back, a puzzled expression on his face. "Sammy?"

"Yes, Teddy?"

"Did you do something to your hair? You look a little different tonight."

SAM AND MURPHY were still laughing when they pulled into her driveway ten minutes later.

"What can I say?" Sam managed between whoops of laughter. "The men in my family aren't terribly observant."

Murphy threw his head back and howled at that one. "He's a cop, Sam! The man's *paid* to be observant."

Sam held her aching sides. "He still can't tell his own twins apart."

"Identical?"

"Not really," said Sam, as her laughter returned anew. "One's a boy and one's a girl."

They laughed until tears came, until Sam was certain it was impossible to laugh anymore and continue to breathe. This was the Murphy O'Rourke she'd first come to know and like. Easy-going, quick to anger and quick to laugh, arrogant, opinionated and—

A man. He wasn't her brother or her father or simply her friend. Tonight the sexual chemistry Caroline had claimed they lacked burst fullblown into being. And as their laughter died, that chemisty reappeared in the quiet of the car.

"Come here." Murphy's voice was low and gruff.

"I have to go in."

"You will," he said, drawing her close to him on the bench seat. "But first we have some old business to settle. I'd like to kiss you once without interruption."

The kiss was longer, deeper, sweeter than the kisses that had come before. Sam felt as if she were floating freely through space and time on a cloud of pure, intense emotion, unlike anything she'd experienced before. And it wasn't simply desire flooding her senses, although that was a part of it. It was something much more complex—and much more dangerous.

"I have to go in," she managed at last.

"Coward," he said. He got out of the car and walked around to open her door.

It was a wonder she managed to walk up the steps, with her head so high in the clouds.

"Sleep well, Sam," he said at the door, after another long and luscious kiss. "I'll be back at eight."

Seven and a half hours, she thought as she watched him drive off down the street.

Her brain told her that Murphy O'Rourke wouldn't be around forever, that his type of man moved on long before life had a chance to get dull.

Her heart told her otherwise.

It had been ages since Sam had listened to her heart but it appeared she had no choice.

For the moment her heart belonged to Murphy O'Rourke.

Chapter Twelve

"Going out again?" said Bill O'Rourke the next morning.

"That's right." Murphy grabbed for his down jacket and heavy gloves. "How about you?"

"Eight-o'clock mass." Bill put on his hat and scarf and looked at his son. "You should try it some time."

So you're bringing out the heavy artillery today, are you? "No lectures today, okay, Pop? The sun is shining, the birds are singing. It's a great morning. Let's leave it at that." Scotty would be helping out at the bar during the day, and Murphy intended to be back before it got crowded in the evening. His father should have absolutely no cause for complaint.

"Are you seeing Samantha today?"

"I am."

"And you saw her last night?"

"That's right." Murphy zipped up his jacket. "Is there something you want to say, Pop?" *Not that I want to hear it, but at least we should get it out in the open.*

"You still planning to leave when I get back behind the bar full-time?"

"My plans haven't changed."

"Then leave her alone, son."

Murphy's jaw dropped. "What did you say?"

His father rested a hand on Murphy's forearm. "I said, leave her alone. This isn't the kind of woman you walk out on when the fun's over."

His pulse beat heavily in Murphy's right temple. "You're on dangerous ground now, Pop. I'd back off if I were you."

"No."

Murphy stared at his old man.

"You've walked away from people and places and things all your life, Murphy. You're not going to do it with that girl and her daughter. Not while I'm alive."

Murphy slapped his gloves against the palm of his left hand. "Where the hell is this coming from? Have you been talking to my beloved brother again?"

"I don't talk to anyone about it. I'm talking to *you* about it. She's a good kid, Samantha is. Don't go leading her on, then leaving her behind like you've left everything else in your life."

"You make me sound like a real nice guy, Pop. What makes you think you know anything about how I feel?"

"I know what I see, is all. I know what you've always done. She deserves better than halfway measures, Murphy. So does her kid."

On that Murphy was in agreement. Samantha deserved the love and security she'd never found with a man, and Patty deserved the seven-day-a-week father of her dreams. But life didn't always send to you exactly what you needed.

Then again, maybe it did. He thought of Sam and how warm and sweet she had felt in his arms last night, of how they had both seemed sprinkled with stardust, blessed with magic. That counted for something, didn't it?

"Be honest with her," Bill warned as he headed for the front door. "Tell her the way it is with you. Don't lead her on."

You know she doesn't understand the rules, Murphy thought. Another woman might accept the fact that things aren't always forever without being told. He doubted if Samantha Dean was one of them.

He looked at his father and wished there were a way to shatter thirty-six years of barriers and strife in a single instant. He wanted to tell Bill that he didn't know what would happen between Sam and him but he wanted the chance to find out. She made him feel different inside, hopeful and young, in a way he hadn't believed was possible.

"Want a lift to church?" he asked as they left the house.

"Walking's good for the heart," said Bill, turning up the collar of his coat.

"I don't mind driving," said Murphy, wondering why he was pushing the issue.

Bill started down the back stairs then stopped and looked back at his son. "You'll leave," he said sagely. "The minute the right job comes along, you'll be gone quicker than she can ask where you're going."

"You don't know that," said Murphy. "You don't know anything about it."

"Maybe not," said Bill with a shrug of his shoulders, "but I know you. You'll leave. Mark my words on that—sooner or later, you'll leave."

WHEN MURPHY O'ROURKE pulled into their driveway at exactly eight o'clock in the morning, Patty nearly swooned with delight. Not only was he handsome and funny and smart, he was punctual, to boot! The only thing that kept him from being absolutely perfect was the fact that his nephew was a whiney little six-year-old who cried for his mother the whole way through the Lincoln Tunnel.

At first she wanted to give the little boy her most withering grown-up glance and tell him he was acting like a baby, but then she suddenly remembered little Kevin might one day be her very own cousin and she reached over and held the child's hand in hers until they came out of the tunnel and into the bright sunlight of Manhattan.

Her Grandma Betty said New York City was a dirty and disgusting place where nobody in his right mind would go unless he absolutely *had* to. Patty had only been to New York City two times in her entire life— once to go to the circus, and, once to see *CATS* on a school outing—but each time she had found it thrilling!

Manhattan was exotic and loud and a million times more exciting on a sleepy Sunday than Rocky Hill was on New Year's Eve. Even the air smelled different in New York City. Eagerly she began to unroll the window only to have her mom's sharp voice stop her in her tracks.

"Keep that window up, young lady," Sam warned. "This isn't Rocky Hill."

As if Patty could forget! She held her breath as two men in torn pants and big, bulky overcoats approached the car and spit on the windows.

Next to her, little Kevin let out a shriek and covered his eyes. Patty stared out at the men as they wiped the spit off with rags made of torn T-shirts.

"Why are they doing that?" she asked Murphy who was reaching into his pockets.

"Money," he said, extracting a few coins. He unrolled his window the tiniest crack and handed each man some change.

"Are they homeless?" she asked. It was hard to imagine why else someone would want to make a living waiting for cars to come out of the tunnel so he could clean their windows.

"Some are, some aren't," said Murphy, heading across the intersection the second the traffic light changed to green. "They've been doing this since before I was Kevin's age. It's anyone's guess."

Patty twisted around in her seat and looked back as three more men joined the original two and pounced on a big black limousine stuck at the light.

There were so many things to look at, that she wished she had eyes in the back of her head so she wouldn't miss one single thing. She swiveled to face front, just in time to see her mom brush a lock of hair off Murphy's forehead and say something that made him smile in a way Patty loved. Perhaps an extra set of ears wouldn't be a bad idea either, preferably ears that could hear private whispers.

There was some real grown-up stuff going on up there and Patty would gladly give twenty IQ points to know what it was. Actually she had a pretty darned good idea of what was happening: sexual chemistry! She had tried really hard to understand the concept when her Aunt Caroline explained it to her earlier in the week but Einstein's Theory of Relativity had been easier to understand than the mysteries between men and women.

But now she knew. Not that she understood it any better than she did a few days ago, but Aunt Caroline had been one hundred percent about one thing: when you saw it, you knew it! The very air around her mom and Murphy O'Rourke shimmered. The way they looked at each other, the sound of their laughter—little things, yes, but somehow those little things seemed to add up to a lot more than Patty would have imagined.

She looked over at Kevin, who was busy blowing spit bubbles in the space between his missing front teeth.

She still thought Murphy was the most absolutely perfect man to be her father—even if it did mean being related to Kevin!

SAM HANDED OVER a bag of warm, fragrant roasted chestnuts to the smiling tourists from Akron, Ohio.

"And a Merry Christmas to you, too," she said, matching them smile for smile. "Don't forget to see the Lord & Taylor windows!"

"We promise," said the man. "You've been terrific."

She watched them stroll down the street, laughing and eating chestnuts. A street-corner Santa manned the other end of the block, and she grinned as the couple from Ohio dropped money into his red chimney. The tinkling of his bell and his merry "Ho! Ho! Ho!" floated back up the street, mingling with the noise of Sunday traffic and holiday shoppers.

What an absolutely splendid day this was turning out to be! It was no wonder Frank wanted to make certain his stand was there in its usual place, wedding or not, for Sam couldn't imagine a more glorious location to experience a New York City Christmas. That majestic symbol of Manhattan at Yuletide, the Rockefeller Center Christmas tree, was straight ahead, rising up in the middle of the concrete and glass like a twinkling, multi-colored jewel. Trumpeting angels, constructed of glittering white lights, lined the walkways of the Plaza as they had year after year, for longer than Sam could remember. She tilted her head and listened to the merry sounds of music rising up from the ice-skating rink and the equally merry sounds of laughter as eager skaters braved the cold.

How long had it been since she'd felt this way—happy, confident? Out there in the brisk winter air, breathing in the sights and sounds of the holiday season and loving every single minute of it.

Of course, seeing the look of pure bliss upon her daughter's freckled face went a long way toward accounting for the joyous feeling inside Sam's heart. Patty beamed with delight each time she looked at Murphy, and Sam had to admit her daughter's affection seemed to be reciprocated. Who on earth would have imagined the gruff Murphy O'Rourke would have such a tender heart? She hadn't been blind to the patient, loving way he handled his fractious little nephew, moving the boy out of his bad mood with a combination of straight talk and a good-natured sense of humor.

But then, neither had she been blind to the tenderness in his eyes last night. What a devastating combination of opposites he had presented to Sam: heartmelting tenderness blended with a fierce sexuality that set fire to her soul.

She'd lain awake for a long time last night, wondering if the magic they'd experienced was the product of satin dresses the color of sapphires, of opulent velvet masks and the shimmering romanticism of the evening. What about when she was just Sam once more, with her straight dark hair and favorite black sweater, and her penchant for denim rather than diamonds?

She smiled foolishly at the passersby as she thought of the look on Murphy's face this morning when he rang her doorbell. The look in his eyes was the same look she had seen the night before when he held her in his arms. It was for *Sam*, not for her wardrobe or makeup or jewelry anymore than the way her heart quickened at the sight of his slightly crooked grin had anything to do with tuxedos or perfectly barbered hair.

Who would have believed it?

Sam was falling in love.

MURPHY WAS MESMERIZED by the animated figures in the window at Lord & Taylor. One, in particular. A lovely dark-haired Gibson girl in a sapphire blue gown who looked uncannily the way Sam had looked last night at the masquerade ball. That beautiful, fine-boned face. The delicate limbs. The doe eyes with their vulnerable intensity.

He crouched down to look more closely at her and felt a tug on his sleeve.

"Murphy." Patty's solemn, bespectacled face popped up in front of his nose. "Kevin has to go to the bathroom."

Murphy blinked and looked down at the squirmy little boy holding onto Patty's hand. "Do you?"

Kevin nodded. "A lot."

Murphy dragged his hand through his hair. There was a lot less of it since his visit to the barber yesterday morning, and it felt strange to him. He thought for a second. "Okay. No problem. We'll go into Lord & Taylor." Made perfect sense to him.

"Macy's," said Patty. "The men's room is bigger."

Murphy laughed out loud. "And how would you know that?"

"My cousin James told me."

Kevin looked up at his uncle with big hazel eyes. "I want Macy's."

Murphy hadn't been a reporter all those years for nothing. These kids were up to something but since it was Christmastime—and he was definitely in a Christmasy mood—he led them up to Herald Square.

Macy's was jammed to the rafters with shoppers. In just the first two minutes he caught the assorted smells of Chanel No. 5, Brut, pine needles, and ginger-bread, and that was just for starters. He heard Chinese being spoken on his left, Spanish on his right, and the particular blend of English known as Brooklynese all around him. He grinned, feeling right at home. *Only in New York....*

He followed a sales clerk's instructions and found the rest rooms with a minimum of trouble. That solved Kevin's problem and any problem Patty might develop in the near future.

"Okay," he said, when they met up at the water fountain between the two rest rooms, "now what? We can go back to Rock Center and hang out with your mom until she closes for the day. We can go to F.A.O. Schwarz and look at toys even Donald Trump can't afford. We can—"

"Santa Claus," said Patty. "I want to see Santa Claus."

"You're kidding."

She shook her head and her pigtails slapped against her shoulders. "This is Christmastime and I'm a kid, aren't I?"

"Sure you are, but I thought—"

"I have something to ask him," said Patty with a quick glance toward Kevin.

Murphy started to say something about still believing in St. Nick but he remembered his little nephew was the jolly fat man's number one fan. *You're okay, Patty,* he thought as he followed her to the toy department and Santa's workshop. He was the adult. He should have come up with the idea of visiting Santa Claus. But it had been Sam's remarkable little girl who'd thought of it. Her fifty megaton IQ may have been a gift from the gods, but her generous heart came straight from her mother.

The line to see Santa was long. He couldn't remember the last time he saw so many little kids in one place before. Kevin was hyper with excitement and Patty held the kid's hand and pointed out the different elves and, unless Murphy was sorely mistaken, seemed pretty excited herself as they moved closer to the chubby guy in the red suit who received visitors on his velvet throne.

Next to his niece and nephew, Patty was the first kid in years who actually got to him. He'd spent most of his life not even noticing the shorter members of the human population. They spoke another language. Ernie. Big Bird. Oscar the Grouch. Murphy hated feeling stupid and talking to kids usually made him feel that way within ten seconds. It wasn't until his sister had Kevin and Laurie, that he'd begun to feel comfortable with kids and, to his amazement, enjoy their company.

He'd felt comfortable with Patty instantly. She was smart and funny and almost fiercely independent but it didn't take a genius to see there was a little girl hiding behind that very adult persona. "You can't walk out on those two," his father had said that very morning, meaning Sam and her little girl. "Don't make promises you can't keep."

I'm not going to hurt you, kiddo, he thought as he looked at Patty's face, flushed with excitement as she sat upon Santa's knee. *And I'm sure as hell going to do my best to make sure I don't hurt your mother.*

Patty whispered something to Santa and then, to Murphy's surprise, the two of them turned and looked straight at him. Patty whispered something else and her happy smile was warm enough to melt the snows outside. Santa Claus winked at him, then flashed Patty a thumbs-up sign.

Murphy had the strangest feeling his future had just been decided for him.

"BUT I CAN'T!" said Sam as Murphy knelt down in front of her.

"Sure you can." He took her foot and rested it on his lap.

"It's been years since I last did it."

"You know that old saying..." His large hands caressed her ankle and teased her calf.

"This isn't like riding a bike, Murphy."

"It's easier. You can let me do all the work."

"You mean, just go along for the ride?"

"Lean on me. I won't go faster than you can handle."

"I shouldn't."

"Of course you should."

"It's dangerous."

"Not if you're careful."

"You're tempting me, Murphy."

"That's the general idea."

"Oh, why not!" She threw caution to the winds. "Go ahead! Lace those skates up for me and let's join the kids on the ice."

WHAT A BEAUTIFUL CITY, Sam thought a half-hour later as Murphy guided her around the skating rink. Fun City. The Big Apple. The most glorious, glamorous place in the entire world at Christmastime and she was right there in the middle of the excitement.

"You're doing great, Sam." Murphy eased them into a gentle turn, all to the rhythm of a Strauss waltz floating from the loudspeakers. "Next thing you know, you'll be going for Olympic Gold."

Sam laughed then grabbed his hand more tightly as her feet threatened to slip out from under her. "I don't think Dorothy Hamill is in any danger. I'm just trying to stay off my keister."

"Hold on to me."

She looked up at him, her heart so filled with emotion she could scarcely breath. "That's what I intend to do."

PATTY AND KEVIN were over in the far end of the rink with the skating instructor.

"Now, start with your right foot and push off—"

Patty started to skate with the rest of the kids when her mom and Murphy glided gracefully by. "Hey!" said Kevin, who was holding her hand. "You almost tripped me!" Patty scarcely heard his words. All of her concentration was focused on the wonderful sight before her. Her mom's cheeks were rosy with the cold and excitement; her dark eyes glowed as she looked up at Murphy and laughed. She didn't look like the glamorous movie star who'd gone to the masquerade last night, but she looked young and pretty and—

In love.

Could it be?

And then Patty saw it, the one thing she'd been waiting all her life to see. Right there in the middle of the ice-skating rink at Rockefeller Center with the Christmas tree twinkling above them, her mom and Murphy O'Rourke kissed each other on the lips, and her cautious, careful mom didn't even care that a million people were watching them!

This was it, she just knew it. This was how it would be if she and her mom and Murphy were a real family, and this was just one of a billion Christmases they'd spend together.

"Come on, guys," said Murphy a few moments later when he and her mom skated up to Patty and Kevin. "We're going to the Automat for dinner."

"The Automat?" asked Patty. "What's that—a carwash?"

"Where have you been keeping this kid?" Murphy asked Sam, giving a playful tug to one of Patty's braids. "The Automat's an American original. You haven't lived until you've had one of their tuna salad sandwiches on white bread."

Sam groaned. "My daughter's tastes are a bit more advanced than that."

"I know the Automat," Kevin piped up. "You stick money in and food pops out the window."

"You remember," said Sam, smoothing Patty's bangs. "Like in that Doris Day movie we saw a few weeks ago, the one with Cary Grant and the New York Yankees."

Twinkling angels with trumpets held high.

A glittering Christmas tree straight out of a fairy tale.

Ice skaters twirling by as gracefully as ballerinas while wonderful music wafted through the air.

Macy's and Lord & Taylor and a Santa Claus who actually made Patty wonder if she should rethink her position on the possibility of flying through the air with eight reindeer and a well-stocked sleigh; and now the Automat where you inserted your coins into a slot

and instead of a game of Pac-Man, you found yourself with hot chocolate and a tuna sandwich!

She glanced at her mom and Murphy, who were
both looking goofier and more lovesick by the minute. This was even better than she had planned.

Chapter Thirteen

"Murphy!" Sam giggled as Murphy maneuvered her into the kitchen at Fast Foods for the Fast Lane. "What if someone sees us?"

Murphy pinned her against the refrigerator and kissed her soundly. "The only way the crowd out there would notice is if the food runs out."

Sam leaned her forehead against his shoulder as a wave of pure pleasure rippled through her body. "Did you know they were planning this?"

Murphy shook his head. "Only thing I knew was to keep you away until they unloaded the supplies."

The masquerade ball had turned out to be only the beginning of the wonderful changes in Sam's life. Christmas was in the air, and so it seemed was magic. There was Murphy, of course, and the joy she felt each time she saw him—not to mention the look of sheer happiness on Patty's face whenever she saw them together. And if that wasn't terrific enough, her father, cousins Teddy and Frank and assorted uncles had commandeered the storefront to perform a little magic of their own. In the next three days they intended to transform her shop into a surefire winner with fresh paint, spanking new wallpaper, and a ceramic tile floor to die for. Sam had only to fill her cupboards and stock her refrigerator and she was ready for business.

She sighed deeply. "Can you believe it?" she said, looking up at Murphy. "I actually have time on my hands."

He waggled his eyebrows in a deliciously wicked way. "I can think of a number of ways to use that time, Samantha."

She lowered her gaze to his mouth. "So can I, Murphy."

SAM SOON DISCOVERED there was any number of delightful ways to spend her free time.

She made Patty country breakfasts then drove her to school each morning. Caroline took to stopping by on her way to work for coffee and conversation, and Sam could barely restrain herself from throwing her arms around her best friend and pledging eternal fealty. If Caroline had not railroaded Sam into going to the masquerade ball, Sam and Murphy might still be having snowball fights in the parking lot.

Not that they were suddenly above snowball fights, mind you. She and Murphy had enjoyed a down-and-dirty battle right in her front yard just the other night. The only problem was that even though she had time to spare, time alone with Murphy was almost impossible to come by. She had her responsibilities toward Patty and her family. He had the bar to take care of. By the time the bar closed well after midnight, Sam was calling it a day.

And so they found stolen moments for long and lingering kisses, but those moments only left her hungry for the taste and smell and feel of him. She had no experience at all in juggling a social life and a family life and the notion of staying out an entire night—even if her mother took care of Patty—was as alien to Sam as the notion of flying to Saturn under her own steam.

Her personal code of behavior had been formed a long time ago and she was comfortable with it. To his credit, Murphy didn't push her to give more than she could, even though she knew he wanted her as much as she wanted him.

She was an old-fashioned woman in a world that held little store in old-fashioned values. She had made love with Ronald Donovan because her heart and soul had belonged to him; because she'd believed she would grow old alongside him. As deep as her feelings were for Murphy, she couldn't delude herself into believing he would still be around when her hair started to turn gray. Paris called to him—and Beijing and London and other exotic cities around the world. She needed more than a few nights in his arms. She would rather never be with him than love him and then lose him to his career.

But in the darkness of her room, alone in her bed, her imagination soared. It was a simple task to conjure up the image of his bare chest as it had looked that first morning she went to O'Rourke's. Every muscle, from his stomach to his shoulders to his biceps, had been imprinted on her memory. She lingered on each one, ran her tongue along the tracing of vein at the bend in his arm, buried her nose where his arm met his shoulder, let her hands slide over his ribcage and down to the round, muscular buttocks.

She knew how he would feel as he covered her body with his. She knew how she would open for him, welcoming him with all her heart and soul. In the quiet heart of the night she could hear the sounds of passion, catch the hot, heavy scent of sexuality, taste herself on his lips—

But she needed more in the way of forever than he could possibly give and they both knew it.

And so they spent their time talking and kissing and talking some more, as the days before Christmas disappeared one by one. Central New Jersey had another snowfall, and if the weather stayed cold they planned to take Patty and Kevin ice-skating Sunday at the pond in Cranbury, a picture-postcard town not far from Rocky Hill.

With all that extra time, also came the opportunity to spend some of it at O'Rourke's with Murphy and the rest of the gang. Instead of carting the sandwiches and appetizers over there on trays as she had in the beginning of their arrangement, she began cooking right on the premises. Bill O'Rourke had settled on an ex-sailor named Donahue to be their full-time cook; he would begin the day after Christmas. Sam intended to take full advantage of her position of power while she could.

Scotty deemed himself her helper and they laughed and joked while Murphy tended the bar. She loved the brilliant professor. He had taken an interest in Patty, confirming what she'd been told since her little girl was old enough to form her first thoughts: Patty's potential was unlimited.

"I'd like the chance to work with her on some mathematical concepts," said Scotty one afternoon in the week before Christmas. "Perhaps after school?"

Sam hugged him and laughed at Murphy's raised eyebrows. "That's wonderful! I'll pick her up this afternoon, and we can put you two at a table in the back of the bar."

"Great," muttered Murphy, with a twinkle in his eye. "I can hear my father now—what the hell are you doing, boy? This is a bar not a nursery school . . ."

"You don't know me as well as you think you do," came a voice from the bottom of the rear staircase. "You bring that little girl of yours around later," Bill O'Rourke said to Sam, after he kissed her on the cheek. "Anything to keep this old Scotsman out of trouble."

Murphy turned away and Sam's heart went out to him. It hadn't taken her long at all to determine that the relationship between the O'Rourke men was complicated, to say the least. Murphy had grown up without the loving support of a mother, and the three men—Murphy, his father and his brother—each donned an impenetrable shield to protect himself from the pain that came with being a family.

And yet she had seen Murphy with her daughter and his nephew, seen the easy-going way he'd handled both their tears and their laughter, felt the warmth and affection that seemed as natural to him as breathing. He would make a tremendous father some day. It was no wonder Patty had been drawn to him from the start.

"Your burger's ready." She garnished the plate with a semicircle of pickle rounds and a sprig of parsley, then handed it to Murphy. "Eat up. You may never see its like again once Popeye starts work here." It was a brilliant burger, if she did say so herself, with two types of cheese melted over the top, sliced red onions, and three strips of perfectly-grilled bacon.

He forced a laugh and for an instant she saw through his gruff exterior and straight to the center of his heart.

"Thanks, Sam," he said. "I could get used to having you around.

Her own heart fluttered dangerously. "Sorry," she said, "but you wouldn't want to disappoint Mr. Donahue, would you?"

Murphy was more wonderful than she'd ever imagined a man could be. To think that ten days ago they had been strangers—the footloose reporter and the earthbound mother and entrepreneur. It never should have worked between them and yet it had, beautifully! He had become a part of her life in the blink of an eye, and with each day that passed she found it increasingly difficult to remember what her life had been like before she met him.

Life seemed brighter, happier, more filled with promise than it had since she was a teenager. Her entire family was still buzzing over the Christmas lights she'd strung in the blue spruce tree in front of her tiny house and the mistletoe and holly she'd scattered about her living room. "Don't you know it's Christmas?" she'd asked Patty when her little girl questioned the pine boughs draped across the mantel and the shimmering ornaments nestled amidst the greenery.

And Sam didn't have to look far to discover the reason for her metamorphosis. Murphy.

Sam's world lit up whenever Murphy O'Rourke entered the room. It was as simple as that.

The delivery man showed up with that week's shipment of beer, and Murphy, hamburger in hand, went off to take care of business. Bill O'Rourke, however, stayed behind.

"How are you feeling?" Sam asked, putting together a low-cholesterol sandwich for him. "I must say you're looking well."

"I'm getting there," said Bill, his lean face creasing in a smile, "but I'm worried."

"I would think that's natural after all you've been through the past couple of months."

He waved his hand in the air between them. "Not about that. I'm worried about you."

"Me? Why on earth would you be worried about me?" This was the happiest time of her adult life. Worry seemed as far away as the twenty-fifth century.

He gestured toward Murphy who was laughing with the delivery man on the opposite side of the bar room. "You like him, don't you?"

Sam, never one to mince words, nodded. "Very much."

"He likes you, too."

She felt her cheeks flame, the same way Patty's did. "I'm pleased."

Bill's hazel eyes, so like Murphy's own, clouded over with sympathy. "The thing is, he won't be around forever."

She touched Bill's forearm in a gentle warning to tread softly through treacherous waters. "Neither will

I. I open my store on January first. We'll have to rearrange our schedules."

"That's not what I'm talking about, Samantha. He's been running since the day he was born and he's not about to stop running now."

"I understand that, Bill. I wouldn't ask that of him any more than he would ask me to abandon my catering shop." Especially not now, when she was on the brink of spreading her wings.

Bill, however, was deep in his own thoughts, caught up in an entire web of family history. "The offer came in."

Sam's breath caught. "I know about the *Telegram*." She'd met Dan Stein on one of his frequent visits down to the wilds of New Jersey to woo Murphy back to the Big City.

"Not the *Telegram*, Samantha."

"The foreign beat?" Her voice was a whisper.

"The foreign beat." Bill patted her shoulder awkwardly. "Looks like we might be saying good-bye to our boy before we know it."

THAT EVENING, Sam, Caroline and Patty sat around the dining room table. Newspaper clippings were scattered everywhere, along with photocopies of magazine articles. In a perfect example of bad timing, Patty had taken it upon herself to do some library research on her favorite topic: Murphy O'Rourke.

"Isn't it wonderful!" Patty's face glowed with excitement. "He's as famous as Bruce Springsteen."

"I wouldn't go that far," said Sam. But there was no mistaking the power of his prose. Murphy

O'Rourke was a well-respected, hard-working member of the Fourth Estate.

"Look at this." Caroline slid a photocopy of a *People* magazine article toward Sam. "He was the main interview in this piece on the Iran-Contra hearings."

"And he was on *Nightline*," Patty sighed. "He met Ted Koppel!"

Only Sam's little girl could wax equally enthusiastic over The Boss and late night TV's version of Howdy Doody.

"He's brilliant," said Caroline.

"He's adorable," said Patty.

"He has what it takes to be the Walter Cronkite of the print world."

"He could be on television."

"He could be the White House correspondent."

"He could win a Pulitzer Prize!"

Sam looked at her daughter and her eyes filled with tears. *Oh, honey, don't you see what this means?* Murphy O'Rourke was all of those things, but the one thing he wasn't was a bartender in Rocky Hill, looking for a wife and daughter who wanted nothing more than to stay exactly where they were.

"YOU REALIZE my family's going to talk about this, don't you?"

"You mean they stop eating long enough for conversation?"

Sam laughed as she turned the Blazer into the parking lot of Quakerbridge Mall a few nights later. "We *do* think about food a lot, don't we?"

"Think about it? Did you see the pile of wrappers Teddy and Frank left behind yesterday? You'll turn a profit just from your family alone."

Sam zeroed in on a space near J. C. Penny's, then muttered something un-Christmaslike as a woman in a blue Volkswagen zipped in ahead of her. "This is disgusting. I think the nearest empty parking spot is in Pennsylvania."

"What do you expect, Sam? It's ten days before Christmas."

"I usually wait until Christmas Eve then run out and do all my shopping in one fell swoop."

"Great attitude, Scrooge."

She screeched to a halt in front of Macy's. "Did Patty tell you about that?"

His expression was blank. "Tell me what?"

"Scrooge. That's my nickname."

"You're kidding."

She shook her head and whipped into a parking space a cool hundred feet from the door. "I'm afraid my Christmas spirit has been conspicuously absent these past few years."

"You seem pretty spirited to me."

She glanced at him. He wasn't laughing. "Sometimes it takes a swift kick in the seat of your pants to make you appreciate life again."

He reached across and took her hand in his. "I know, Sam."

How handsome he looked in the dim light of the truck. The right side of his rugged face was in shadow; the left was illuminated by the refracted glow from the streetlamp. Sharp angles and planes; hazel eyes that warmed her with a look—had there really been a time when Murphy O'Rourke had been a stranger to her life?

Moments like these were dangerous, however. Moments like these led deeper into the darker terrain of the heart, a place where Sam had little experience.

"Come on, Murphy," she said, pulling her shopping list out of her pocket. "Let's hit the mall." The only danger there was to her bank balance.

SAM WAS MANY THINGS: a terrific mother, beautiful woman and budding business genius in the making, but she was one lousy shopper. It took Murphy exactly six minutes and forty-five seconds to discover just how lousy.

"You need a plan," he said, forcing her to sit down on a bench in front of Hahne's. "Give me your list."

"Mind your own business, O'Rourke."

"I won't have a chance if you keep us running around in circles all night. Let's attack this scientifically."

"Spoken just like a man," she said, her dark brown eyes twinkling. "I suppose you know everything there is to know about Christmas shopping."

"I know how to get it done with a minimum of trouble."

"I thought trouble was half the fun of Christmastime."

"You're baiting me, Ms Scrooge."

She batted her eyelashes at him. "Now whatever do you mean, Mr. O'Rourke?"

He grabbed her list and scanned it quickly, looking for his name.

Sam grabbed the list back. "Don't look at that!"

"I already did. I'm not on the list."

He must have looked embarrassingly dejected, because she laughed and kissed him, right there in the middle of Quakerbridge Mall. "I don't need a list, Murphy. I know exactly what I'm getting you for Christmas."

He grinned. "You do?"

"I do."

"Will I like it?"

She paused, obviously considering his question. "I'm reasonably sure you will."

"Animal, vegetable, or mineral?"

"Sorry, Murphy. It's a surprise."

He leaned over and whispered something in her ear and she blushed, but looked pleased.

"Amazing," she whispered. "How did you ever guess?"

"Wishful thinking, Sam," he said, counting the days until Christmas. "Wishful thinking."

It was eight days before Christmas. Murphy was getting ready to take Sam and Patty to the McCarter Theater to see a Princeton theater group's version of *A Christmas Carol*. He was feeling a little like Scrooge himself. Dan Stein had called twice, pushing Murphy to take the job on the *Telegram* and issuing dire warnings about some "...young Turk..." who was ready, willing and able to take Murphy's place if he didn't make up his mind and soon.

And then there was UPI. They'd sweetened their offer again, tossing in perks that would make another man weak at the knees.

He reached for his tie and draped it around his neck. Although he must have tied a thousand ties in his life, his fingers fumbled for a second before mechanical memory took over.

Another man, however, didn't have Samantha Dean to consider. Another man didn't have a brilliant little girl with bright red hair to think about.

He stared at his reflection in the mirror as he straightened the knot and smoothed the collar of his shirt. He remembered the exact time and place when he bought that shirt. A stormy May afternoon in Paris with a Frenchwoman with laughing eyes by his side. Whatever happened to her? Did she walk beside another foreign correspondent now and show him the best places to eat and the best places to drink and the best places to buy his shirts?

He wanted that old life on the foreign beat.

He wanted the down-and-dirty excitement of working on the *Telegram* in New York City.

And, damn it to hell, he wanted the happiness he'd found right there in Rocky Hill, in the arms of his Sam.

Bill's warnings came back to him now, and for the first time he understood. Could he ask Sam to give everything up—everything she'd worked so long and hard to achieve—and fly away with him? Could he ask Patty to live the life of a gypsy, moving from city to city, hotel to hotel, while he pursued his dream?

The answer was in reach. He could smell it and taste it but he couldn't put his finger on it. Not yet. But it was there, waiting for him to figure it out, and he wasn't altogether sure he was going to like that answer once he found it.

"YOU'RE QUIET TONIGHT." Murphy smoothed Sam's dark hair off her cheek and kissed the curve of her jaw. "Thinking about the Ghost of Christmas Past?"

Sam closed her eyes for a moment. It was Christmas Yet To Come that concerned her. "The show was wonderful, wasn't it?"

"Patty seemed to think so."

"My little girl would like Christmas to last all year long."

"Sounds good to me."

Sam looked at him, at his beautiful hazel eyes. "I never thought I'd say this, but it sounds good to me, too. In fact, I wish this Christmas season would never end."

Say something, Murphy. Tell me you love me, that you can't imagine leaving me behind while you conquer London and Paris and Rome.

Of course Murphy said nothing like that. He couldn't, because those words weren't part of him. His heart was torn with love and fear and doubt, all the crazy, wild emotions he'd hoped he'd seen the last of. He wanted everything, Murphy did. He wanted lover and wife. He wanted home and adventure. He wanted everything, and he didn't know what he could give in return.

And of course Sam didn't pursue the answer, because deep in her heart she knew she didn't really want to know.

But it was there, hovering between them, like Marley's Ghost, and it wouldn't go away.

"BACK EARLY."

Murphy started at the sound of his father's voice and reached for the kitchen light switch. "Why are you sitting in the dark? We're earning enough money to pay the electric bill, Pop.''

Bill was seated at the head of the kitchen table with a cup of warm milk in front of him. "I was thinking about your mother.''

Murphy said nothing as he crossed the room toward the refrigerator. What he wanted was a Scotch, straight up. What he had was orange juice straight from the carton. He sat down next to his father and took a long gulp. "Anything in particular about my mother?''

Bill sighed and shrugged his shoulders. "Just that I loved her, and it wasn't enough to make a difference.'' Murphy's mother had died in an accident before Murphy was old enough to start school.

"You always loved her, didn't you?'' Murphy asked. His questions surprised him. He usually did a 180-degree turn away from conversations like this.

"From the first moment.''

"You gave up that job with the Navy to marry her.''

His father's eyes widened. "How'd you know that?''

It was Murphy's turn to shrug. "I don't know. It seems as if I've always known it.'' He leaned toward his father. "Was it a hard decision?''

Bill looked at him as if he were speaking in tongues. "Hard?''

"Yeah.'' *Tell me, Pop. I need your help this time.* "Did you ever wonder if you made the right decision?''

"Never.'' Bill's eyes filled with tears. "Not even for a second.''

Murphy fell silent. It seemed as if he'd been filled with questions and doubts his entire life, always wondering if something better, something more exciting waited around the next corner. Something that would finally make his father sit up and notice him.

"You're not for her," said Bill, breaking the heavy silence of the kitchen.

"I think you're wrong," said Murphy. "I can make her happy. I can take her places she's never been."

"She's not like you. She's making her life here."

"She won't have financial problems anymore. The pressure will be off."

"She's the marrying kind, Murphy. Make no mistake about that. She has a daughter and a family and a future to consider, with or without you. She got along fine without you all these years, and she'll be fine again, if you get out now."

Murphy looked down at his hands. He wanted everything. He wanted Sam and Patty and the life he used to have. "How the hell do I decide?" he asked his father. "How do I know the right thing to do?"

Bill O'Rourke looked at him long and hard. "Son," he said, his eyes sad and old, "if you have to ask, then you don't know the answer."

THIS WAS EVERYTHING Patty had ever wanted in her whole entire life.

It was six days before Christmas, and she was curled up in the back seat of her mom's Blazer, right next to a big beautiful fresh-cut pine tree that smelled exactly the way a Christmas tree ought to smell. Normally her mom insisted on a fake tree because it was easier and could be shoved away back in the basement with no

fuss the second the holidays were over. Murphy, however, shared Patty's belief that Christmas meant tradition, and he led them over to a Christmas tree farm
in Hopewell where she and her mom watched while he
huffed and puffed and chopped one down especially
for her.

Her mom had finally stopped being Mrs. Scrooge.
Murphy was a part of both of their lives. Professor
Scotty had volunteered his time and expertise to teach
Patty the advanced theories only Princetonians of his
caliber were privy to. Hidden away in her coat pocket
were two matching keychains she'd bought at the mall,
halves of the same heart, one inscribed "Mom" and
the other, "Murphy."

Life was about as wonderful as it was possible to be,
and she had Career Day at Harborfields School to
thank for it! And although Patty was too old and too
smart to believe in such things, the little girl part of her
heart couldn't help but pray that the wish she'd whispered in the ear of the Macy's Santa Claus would
come true on Christmas morning and she would wake
up to discover that Murphy O'Rourke was going to be
her dad.

"WHERE DO YOU WANT IT?" Murphy's voice was
muffled from under the boughs of the pine tree.

"In the living room," Sam called, grabbing the bags
of ornaments out of the Blazer and closing the tail-
gate. "Right near the picture window."

Patty climbed out of the back, looking green around
the gills.

"Are you okay, honey?" Sam asked, feeling her
forehead.

"My stomach hurts."

Sam chuckled. "It's no wonder after all those hot dogs you ate over at the Market Fair. Let's go inside and I'll make you a cup of tea." She followed her daughter into the house. "Go check on the Christmas tree," she told Patty as she headed toward the kitchen. "I don't know if Murphy's up to the Dean standards of holiday decorating."

Patty disappeared down the hallway toward the living room. Sam put the packages on the counter top and slipped out of her coat. Hot chocolate, that was the ticket. She'd make a nice pot of it and toast some bread and—

"Sam."

She looked up. Murphy stood in the doorway, an odd expression upon his face.

"Is something wrong?" She stepped from around the counter. "Patty. Is she—"

"Patty's okay. There's someone here to see you."

A man appeared at Murphy's side. A man with bright blue eyes and deep red hair and a smile she knew as well as she knew her own.

"Hello, Samantha. It's been a long time."

It was Ronald Donovan.

The father of her child.

Chapter Fourteen

Patty sniffled and reached for the tissue on her night-stand. She had cried her way through one entire box and was well on her way to using up a second one, since her biological father left a few hours ago.

If she lived to be an old lady with no teeth and a hearing aid, she'd never, absolutely *never* forget the look on her mom's face when Captain Donovan said he wanted to take Patty away with him.

He was a stranger! Oh, sure, she'd seen him once or twice when she was a real little girl but those visits hadn't amounted to more than a pat on the head and a present wrapped up by some clerk in the department store at Quakerbridge Mall. "Give me something little girls like," he would have said, taking out his wallet. "You be the judge." If she closed her eyes she could still see the chubby girl cherubs and little boy angels on that "Welcome, new baby!" paper wrapped around her birthday present.

Why didn't he just go away wherever it was he came from? Why should she be punished because he got married and had a little boy of his own and suddenly decided he wanted to be her father, too?

She wished she didn't have his red hair and blue eyes. She wished she looked just like her mother and could pretend that Captain Donovan never existed—just like he'd spent so many years pretending his own daughter had never existed.

"I can give Patricia things you couldn't hope to provide, Captain Donovan had said after Murphy said good-night. *The finest private schools, tutors...think about it, Samantha. Are you being fair to the child?"*

Patty buried her face in her arms as deep sobs wracked her body. Didn't anybody understand that she was just like other ten-year-old girls? Didn't anybody understand that being smart didn't mean she didn't want the same things all of her friends wanted?

She didn't care about private schools and tutors and the fancy clothes and computers that Captain Donovan thought were so important for her to have. She wanted to stay right here with her mom and Murphy O'Rourke and be part of a *real* family.

All of her friends had moms and dads and sisters and brothers and arguments over who got to use the bathroom next. That's what she prayed to God for each night. That's the wish she wished over her birthday candles and looked for in every fortune cookie she opened.

It wasn't that much to ask. Why didn't her mom and Murphy O'Rourke understand that all they had to do was get married and all of her wishes would come true.

MURPHY GULPED DOWN a whiskey back at the bar and ignored the questioning look on Scotty's face. He hated Air Force Captain Ronald J. Donovan, Jr. The moment he saw the guy standing there, tall and straight and arrogant in his dress blues, it had taken the better part of valor to keep Murphy from ramming his fist down the guy's throat.

"Who the hell does he think he is, showing up like that?" he growled, storming back and forth. "Who the hell shows up ten years later to claim his kid?"

It's not your business. She's not your kid. Sam's not your wife.

"He looks like a damn jerk," he said to Scotty without explanation. "Arrogant, smug. Who the hell does he think he is?"

Scotty opened his mouth to speak but Bill placed a hand on the man's shoulder and met his son's eyes.

"Can you do better for her, son? What can you offer her that he can't?"

"I don't know!" Murphy roared. "All I know is I can't stand what's going on."

He wasn't afraid Sam would run off with her first love. Donovan was married with a kid and a career and plans for the future—a future that included Patty. It was something else that ate away at his gut, something darker and more frightening. That terrible thought that maybe the best thing that had ever happened to him was slipping through his hands.

"You gotta make up your mind to get out of her life, boy. For once in your life don't do what's best for you."

"It's not that easy," Murphy muttered, pouring himself another whiskey. Sam had done a fine job, bringing up her kid before either Murphy or Ronald Donovan showed up at her doorstep. Patty was bright and funny and endearing, and any man who became her twenty-four-hour-a-day dad would be one lucky guy. "He doesn't want Sam. He wants their kid."

His father put an arm around Murphy for the first time in a good twenty years. "It's not your decision, son. You don't have the right to an opinion this time around."

SAM WAS DETERMINED that the presence of Ronald Donovan in their lives wouldn't change things, and she embraced wrapping packages and decorating the Christmas tree with almost missionary zeal. She whirled through the small house like a tornado, making certain she stayed one full step ahead of the panic that waited at the outer edges of her mind.

"Over there!" She pointed toward a bare branch near the top of the tree. "The silver angel goes right next to the sleigh bells."

Murphy, who had been oddly quiet that evening, looped an ornament hanger through the angel's wings and positioned it on the tree. "How's that?"

"Terrific." *Right word, Sam. Where's the spirit to go with it?* Things had been so wonderful these past few weeks. She wasn't going to let Ronald Donovan's belated interest in fatherhood ruin the happiness she'd found with Murphy—and she sure wasn't going to let him ruin Patty's Christmas.

Murphy turned away from the tree, and she felt his gaze on her. "Are you okay, Sam?"

"Wonderful!" She forced a laugh. "Back to work, O'Rourke. If we want to get this finished before Patty comes home from math class, we have our work cut out for us."

"Let's take a break."

She shook her head.

"Sam." He moved closer and took her hand. "How bad is it?"

She lowered her head so he wouldn't see the hunted expression she knew was on her face. "Awful. He wants Patty to live with him this summer."

He was quiet for a moment. "That doesn't sound so terrible. Yeah, you'll miss her but isn't this what you wanted for her?"

"No." The force of her word surprised both of them. "I want a father for her, Murphy, not a caretaker. She needs love, not an unlimited expense account."

"Then your answer should be pretty clear."

"It's not that simple." The truth was that Ronald was offering Patty more than a summer; he was offering her a world of possibilities. She blinked away tears of confusion, then looked up at Murphy. "He can give Patty everything she deserves, Murphy—tutors and computers and the best schools in the country. I can't give her anything more than Rocky Hill and an uncertain future."

Was she wrong or did he flinch at her words?

"I know all about uncertain futures," he said slowly, his words measured. "I still don't know where I'll be come New Year's." He didn't have to say the next words; they both heard them loud and clear inside their hearts: *Not much of a life for a child . . .*

"Ronald asked me how you figured in our lives."

Murphy's smile was quick and bittersweet. "And . . . ?"

"I don't know how, Murphy," she said at last. "Do you?"

They had friendship on their side; they had respect, and chemistry, and—just maybe—they had love.

The one thing they didn't have was one chance in a thousand to make it work.

"I'M SORRY," Sam said to Ronald on his fourth day in town. "Patty's still at school."

"I know. I want to speak with you, Samantha."

She stepped aside and motioned him into her house. Did the man sleep in his uniform? This was their third encounter and she had yet to see him in civilian clothes. No matter how hard she looked, she couldn't find the boy she'd once loved anywhere in the man who stood before her now.

"Coffee?" She led him into the living room and gestured for him to take a seat.

"Nothing, thank you." He stood at attention, and it took Sam a moment to realize he was waiting for her to sit down before he took a seat.

She toyed with the idea of never sitting down for the rest of her life, but decided not even Patty would be this silly, and she perched on the arm of the wing chair. "Are you still taking Patty to dinner the day after tomorrow?"

"Yes," said Ronald, sitting down on the center cushion of the couch. "Linda will be joining us."

"With the baby?"

He shook his head. "My family will watch him."

Okay. So much for conversational gambits. "What is it you want, Ronald?"

He reached into one of his pockets and withdrew a sheaf of papers with razor-sharp creases, then handed them to Sam. ''The best school for advanced students in the country.''

Sam's hand shook visibly as she accepted the papers and placed them in her lap. ''I'll give this to Patty.''

''I want you to read it.''

''I'd rather not.''

''It concerns Patricia's best interests.''

''I think I'm a fairly good judge of Patty's best interests, Ron.''

''Perhaps not when it comes to her future.''

Sam stood up, anger heating her blood. ''You've already missed ten years of her past.''

''And I'm trying to make amends.''

''I don't need your help.''

''I'm not offering any help to you, Samantha. This is for my daughter.''

''*My* daughter, Ron. You don't have any claim over her.''

''You have a right to hate me.''

''I don't hate you. You just don't figure in my life at all.'' *And I don't want you suddenly turning my daughter's life inside out.*

''Now that I have Linda and little Thomas, I understand what I've missed.''

''How wonderful for you.''

''I'm not looking to take Patricia away from you.''

Sam couldn't speak as panic grabbed her by the throat and wouldn't let go.

''All I am asking of you, Samantha, is the right to give Patricia the things you cannot.''

"Like what, Ron? Love? Security? A hometown?"

"An education."

She stopped. This was dangerous territory, the one area she'd yet to master. "She's too young to be sent away to school."

"That may be true for an average child, but there is nothing average about Patricia."

"Only her IQ is unusual, Ron. She's just a little girl."

Ronald stood up, six feet two inches of impressive Air Force blue. "That's the kind of thinking that will limit her horizons." He talked about the exclusive school in northeast Massachusetts that specialized in expanding the horizons of children as gifted as Patty.

I don't like this, Ron. I don't want you to make sense. I want to hate you and your wife and your baby and everything you have to say... The things he was saying were the same things she worried about late at night when her defenses were down and guilt rose swiftly to the surface.

"I want you to think seriously about it," Ronald said, heading for the door. His posture was ramrod perfect; she could have dropped a plumb line straight down from his scalp to his heels. "I would like to broach the topic with Patty at dinner."

"I'll read the brochure but I won't make any other promises. I only want what's best for Patty."

"As do I. You're still a very young woman, Samantha. You've had more than your share of responsibility. Perhaps you and your friend Mr. O'Rourke might have more time to explore your relationship if you didn't have the day-to-day work involved with raising Patricia."

Sam didn't bother to dignify that last remark with an answer. Raising Patty was the single most wonderful experience of her life. "As I said, I'll think about it."

"I can't ask for more than that, can I?"

"No, you can't." *Why then do I have the feeling you will?*

PATTY PRESSED HERSELF up against the kitchen door and listened as Sam walked Captain Donovan out to his waiting cab.

You've had more than your share of responsibility...you and Mr. O'Rourke...more time together without Patricia to care for...

Murphy hadn't come around today. Her mom had lost that Christmas glow, and the tree Murphy had chopped down for them stood forlorn in the corner of the living room, its glittering ornaments looking sad somehow and abandoned.

You know why, a little voice deep inside her whispered. Oh, they tried to hide what was going on, but Patty knew. Grown-ups always said things like "Love isn't always enough," and Patty had never really understood what that meant until now. She knew—she just *knew* her mom and Murphy were as in love as any two grown-ups could possibly be.

But still it wasn't enough to change things.

And it had taken her father, Captain Ronald Donovan, to make her realize that only she could make it all work out for her mom and Murphy O'Rourke.

"YOU'RE DOING the right thing," his father said as he took Murphy to the train station at Princeton Junction on the morning of December 23rd. "It's time you decided what you're going to do."

The choice was what it had been from the beginning, between Dan Stein at the *Telegram* and the chief honcho at UPI. The exhilarating daily grind of a New York daily versus the glamour—and often, loneliness—of the foreign beat. UPI had outdone themselves. It was hard to imagine what reason he could come up with to justify refusing their offer. Money. Position. Perks up the ying-yang. All Dan Stein at the *Telegram* was offering him was hard work, stress, and a 15 point byline.

There didn't seem to be much of a choice.

"You'll be okay at the bar?"

Bill nodded. "I've missed it. Besides we're closed tomorrow night for Scotty's party."

"I'll be back Christmas afternoon."

Bill nodded again. "Did you tell Samantha?"

"What is this—an inquisition?" He'd told Sam, but it seemed to him that his announcement barely registered. She'd looked at him with those big brown eyes and said nothing, and he'd felt as if he'd taken a slam in the solar plexus. "She has a lot on her mind lately."

"You're doing the right thing," said Bill as the train lumbered into the station.

Yeah, Pop. You've already said that.

MANHATTAN that afternoon was one big Christmas party. Murphy dropped in on some of his old pals at City Hall, then strolled over to Wall Street to schmooze with the guys who played Monopoly with real money on a daily basis. Everyone thought him crazy to ever have considered not taking the foreign assignment. "New York?" they said. "Who needs it? Only a lunatic would stay here when Paris calls."

New York was cold in the winter and hot in the summer. It was loud and dirty and often dangerous.

"You'll regret it," said Dan Stein over egg nog at the *Telegram* office. "Hook up with those guys and you'll get fat and soft and forget everything you ever knew about hard-hitting journalism."

"Right," said Murphy. "Like the *Telegram* is going to match their offer."

"Pretty close." Stein quoted a figure.

Murphy whistled. "I'm impressed."

"You should be," said the older man. "Some of that came out of my hide."

"It's tempting but I don't think I'm going to bite."

"You're making a mistake."

"Probably."

"What about that woman with the kid? What happened? I thought you had something pretty special cooking there."

"It's complicated," Murphy said, hedging. "We want different things from life." *How different, moron? You both want to be happy, don't you?*

"Some things you don't walk away from," said Stein. "But I don't suppose you're old enough to realize that yet."

Feeling older by the minute, Murphy popped in at the UPI party a little after six o'clock. He'd expected lights and music and laughter. Good food and better conversation. At the very least, he'd expected a crowd of people bent on having a good time.

What he found was a cleaning woman who looked at Murphy as if he'd escaped from a police lineup.

"Everybody's gone home," she said, making sure her mop was between them. "Don't you have a home?"

He doubled back to the *Telegram* party. Maybe he could con Dan Stein into taking him out to dinner.

"Everyone is gone," said the night receptionist, her brown eyes kind and warm. Like Sam's.

"Did the party move some place else?"

She shook her head. He saw pity on her face. He hated pity. "I'm afraid they all went home."

"Dan Stein's not here?"

"Afraid not."

Murphy ducked into a telephone booth in the lobby and dialed Dan's home number. "Hey, Dan!" he said when his one-time boss picked up the phone. "How about you and the wife and I mixing with the hot-shots at the Russian Tea Room? I know how you like blini and—"

Dan's voice was filled with compassion. Murphy hated compassion more than he hated pity. "We're having a Chanukah celebration tonight. You're more than welcome to join us, kid."

Murphy wanted to join them more than he'd admit even to himself. "That's family time," he said, keeping his voice light. "*Mazel Tov.* I'll talk to you in a couple of days."

The most exciting city in the world was quiet as the grave. Murphy made his way back to the Plaza through a light snowfall. Even the hotel seemed deserted. He went up to his room and ordered a room-service dinner. In his entire life, he couldn't remember a time when he felt more alone.

He missed Sam. That went without saying, for he missed Sam every second he was away from her. He missed Patty almost as much. That was no surprise.

The fact that he missed his father was. He missed Bill's bitching and moaning, his sometimes caustic wit, the nagging sense that they were on the verge of something good after so many years of causing each other nothing but pain.

He missed his sister and his niece and nephew.

And he missed the bar. His pal Scotty with the trenchant humor and steel-trap brain. Joe and Eddy and the other regulars who over the years had made O'Rourke's Bar and Grill into a second home. They were family, all of them, in the truest sense of the word. They were there for each other in hard times; when others turned away, they were still there. They'd been part of Murphy's life since before he could remember. When he swooped into town—hail! the conquering hero—they had opened ranks to let him in but never once did they let success go to his head. He could be O'Rourke the gonzo journalist bigshot away from Rocky Hill, but there in the bar he was Bill's kid.

It was nice to know you had a place in the world.

Tonight in that empty hotel room in that empty city away from everything that mattered, he realized the truth. If he took that job with UPI, this would be his life. He'd live from hotel room to hotel room, his entire world crammed into two battered suitcases and summed up on his passport. He'd been there before and, by God, he'd be damned if he'd be there again.

He'd had it all before, but it hadn't been enough. It still wouldn't be. He could see that now. The fancy career and the fancy salary and all the fancy perks that came with the package could never reach the part of him that only Sam had been able to touch.

And the answer was so damned simple that he could only wonder how it was it had taken him so long to figure it out.

He'd take Dan Stein's offer to return to the *Telegram*. He'd fight the traffic, ride the railroad, live in Rocky Hill the rest of his life—hell, he'd do whatever it was he had to do in order to hold on to Sam and Patty and the family they could form together.

"Some things you don't walk away from," Dan Stein had said earlier that afternoon, and finally Murphy understood exactly what his new/old boss had meant.

It was all there, waiting for him, right where he'd first started out thirty-six years ago.

AT SEVEN on the evening of December 23rd, Ronald came by to pick Patty up for dinner and Sam found it difficult to keep from wrapping her arms around her only child and locking her away in her little house in Rocky Hill.

But of course she didn't. She smiled and said hello to Ronald and kissed Patty good-bye. She even stood on the front stoop and waved as Ronald backed his rented car out of the driveway and disappeared down the street. A light snow had begun to fall an hour ago. "Drive carefully!" she called out before she went inside.

It was out of her hands now. She had read the brochures about the Grey Oaks School. She had digested the impressive paragraphs of information about the Rhodes scholar tutors and state-of-the-art equipment and five-star accommodations. Her eyes had skittered over the hefty price tag attached to this golden opportunity, for Ronald had been one hundred percent right when he said it was beyond her ability to provide.

God knew Patty deserved this opportunity. Just because Rocky Hill fit Sam to a tee, didn't mean Patty would spend her days in the sleepy, historic town. Sam had been an average student, with average needs and average desires—not a little girl with the potential to make a difference in this world.

I miss you, Murphy, she thought as she moved through her empty house. *I wish I could talk to you about this.* But she couldn't. Murphy had left this morning for Manhattan and wasn't expected back until Christmas Day. Right this minute he was probably at some fancy party, drinking champagne and eating caviar, up to his eyeballs in beautiful, brainless blondes.

Her whole world was crumbling around her feet. Ronald was there to woo her daughter away. Murphy couldn't wait to see Rocky Hill in his rearview mirror.

There would be no more long, lingering kisses in the dark. No more whispered fantasies. No more kidding herself that their worlds could possibly coexist and include Patty, as well.

Merry Christmas, she thought, slumping into the recliner and staring at *Wheel of Fortune.*

She'd been right about Christmas all along. It was only for fools looking for a broken heart.

And Sam felt like the biggest fool of them all.

BY THE TIME MURPHY left New York City on the morning of the twenty-fourth, it was snowing in earnest. Big fat flakes obscured his vision from the window of the train bound for Princeton Junction, and the snow showed no sign of letting up. When the train pulled into the station an hour later, at least five inches had fallen, and he considered himself damn lucky to find a cab.

He burst into the bar a little after noon. "Where's Sam?" he called out. "I have to talk to her."

"She left," said Scotty, who was playing a game of gin with Bill. "With the storm and everything, she thought she should get home to Patty."

"What the hell are you doing here?" Bill asked. Murphy peeked at his dad's hand. The old man had three aces sitting side by side. Talk about the luck of the Irish.

"I'm staying," said Murphy, tossing his bags down behind the bar. "I'm taking my old job on the *Telegram*. I'm going to live in Rocky Hill and commute on that lousy railroad if I have to. And I intend to marry Sam if she and Patty will have me. I know what those two need. They need *me*. Sam needs a man who loves her, and Patty needs a father who understands she'll be a genius for the rest of her life, but she'll only be a child a little while longer. I'll be damned if I let her lose the best years of her life!" He stormed over to his father and glared at the man. "If you have a problem with that, keep it to yourself, or you might find me working the bar until the end of my days."

"Don't even kid like that," Bill said. "Go find her. Tell me that my golden years will be peaceful."

"It's all your fault," Murphy ranted, waving a finger under his father's nose. "I'm the product of conditioning. I want a wife, and a kid, and a damn house in the middle of nowhere. Everything I swore I'd never want." He stopped waving his index finger and offered his hand in greeting. "Thanks, Pop. I don't think I'll be able to repay you."

"So what are you waiting for?" his father bellowed. "Go claim your wife."

Murphy disappeared out the door as a big smile appeared on Bill O'Rourke's face.

"You sly dog," said Scotty, shaking his head in amazement. "This is what you wanted all along, isn't it?"

Bill's smile grew wider and he put his cards on the table. "Full house," he said. "Looks like I won the game."

MURPHY WAS A SWEATY, miserable wreck of a man by the time he got to Sam's house. The snow was deep and treacherous. He hated driving in the best of times; this was a trip to Dante's hell. He would have driven through a blizzard, however, to see Sam again and tell her he loved her.

He plowed his way up the unshoveled driveway and stomped up the stairs to the front door. He rang the bell. No answer. He rang again. Still no answer. Her car was there in the driveway. She had to be home.

He tried the doorknob. It was unlocked. Once they were married, he'd have to make sure the doors were locked. "Sam!" His voice seemed to echo in the quiet house. "Sam! Where are you?"

He heard a noise and turned to see her standing in the archway to the hall. Her lovely face was whiter than the snow falling outside. In her hand she held her daughter's Pound Puppy with the torn-off right ear.

"It's Patty," she said, her voice trembling. "She's gone."

Chapter Fifteen

Murphy was beside her before her legs gave way beneath her. He put his arms around her and led her to the sofa then sat down next to her and tried to bring the circulation back into her hands.

"She's gone," Sam repeated, her brain as frozen as the street outside her window. "She's gone!"

Murphy's ruddy face blanched but that was the only indication of fear. "Back up, Sam. Tell me the whole story."

Her hands fluttered helplessly in the air before her and he captured them again between his. "I went to the bar to make lunch. Patty was watching television. She was in her pajamas and robe. I wasn't gone more than an hour—" Her voice broke and she lowered her head in despair. "Oh, God, Murphy!"

"Donovan." Murphy's voice was hard with anger. "If that son of a bitch has kidnapped her, I'll—"

"He wouldn't," Sam said. If she was sure of anything, she was sure of that. "He took her out to dinner last night. If he had kidnapping in mind, he wouldn't have brought her back home."

Murphy glowered in her direction. "Did she leave a note?"

"Nothing."

"Did she pack a suitcase?"

"I didn't look."

They jumped up and ran to Patty's room. As far as Sam could tell, her daughter had taken nothing but her book bag and a few dollars from her piggybank.

"Christmas shopping?" asked Murphy.

"She finished ages ago." Sam couldn't stop the tears from flowing as she met Murphy's eyes. "It's my fault. I thought I was doing the right thing. I want her to have every advantage in the world." The thought of her daughter's sad little face when she came home from dinner with Ronald tore at Sam's heart. "She wondered why you weren't here for the past few days. She thinks she's to blame. She probably thinks I want her to go away."

"Where would she go?"

"I don't know. We can call Susan. My mother. Caroline."

Murphy pushed her toward the phone. "Go ahead. I'll go next door and call my contacts." He hugged her close for an instant, and she felt his strength flow into her body. "We'll bring that girl home, Sam. You can count on it."

One more miracle, God, Sam prayed as she dialed Susan's number. *You gave me Murphy. Now please help us find my little girl.*

MURPHY'S WEB of contacts reached far and wide. Scotty and the crew set out in the blizzard to look for the little girl. He called Sam's cousin Teddy and alerted the local police force and beat reporters from the *Home News*, *Courier*, *Newark Star-Ledger* and the *Trentonian*.

"We'll find her," he said to a crying Sam, after he ran back to her house. "*I'll* find her."

"I'm going with you."

"No!" He sat her back down on the sofa and smoothed her silky hair back from her face. "Not this time. Stay here. She might come back on her own."

"Oh, God, Murphy...the storm! How will she find her way?"

"Trust me." His tone brooked no argument. "I wouldn't let you down. What kind of way would that be to start our future together?"

Future? Sam thought as he ran through the snow to his rented car. *What future?* "Murphy!" Her voice bounced off the snowdrifts and back to her as he disappeared into the storm.

MURPHY'S FINGERS clutched the steering wheel of Sam's four-wheel-drive in a death grip.

"Bad choice of words, O'Rourke," he muttered through the sweat dripping down his face. He'd been out there for hours and still no luck. Visibility was zero. He had no traction; the vehicle slid from side to side as if it were entered in an Olympic ice-skating event. Not even four-wheel-drive was enough to combat the icy undercoating beneath the snow. The only thing he hated more than the act of driving was driving in a blizzard.

Somehow it didn't matter.

He had to find Patty—and not just for Sam. He had to find her for himself, as well.

SAM FELT USELESS back at the house. She had never been good at waiting. She'd always been the type of person to leap into things feet first, rather than hold back and read the instructions.

She smiled despite her panic. That's how it had been with motherhood. She read the books and studied the manuals and asked her own mother a thousand questions, but when it came down to it, she trusted her instincts and she and Patty had done just fine.

Why hadn't she trusted her instincts this time? Ronald was wrong. She understood his position about sending Patty to the best schools possible, but this wasn't the time. She needed to be a little girl first and a genius second. She needed to be grounded in home and family before she faced the world beyond Rocky Hill.

She needed Sam and, God willing, she needed Murphy O'Rourke, as well.

Our future together. She was positive she'd heard him say those words, positive they weren't a figment of her imagination. Oh, dear God, was it so much to ask for, that she and Murphy have a future as a family—and that Patty be right there at the center of it, safe and strong and healthy.

But outside the storm was raging and her little girl was so—

"No!" Sam's voice was loud and strong in the quiet house. Patty was fine. She was probably at school or at the library or off with her Grandma Betty doing some last-minute shopping. *I won't think about anything else,* she vowed. *I absolutely will not!*

She glanced at her watch. Four o'clock. Out on the street her neighbors were setting up the luminaria. As soon as the sky grew dark, the candles would be lighted, turning the entire street into a fantasyland. From babyhood on, Patty had loved sitting on the front steps and watching for that magical moment— even though Sam had never mustered up enough enthusiasm or spare cash to participate herself.

"Come home, Patty," she whispered to the empty room. "It's Christmas Eve."

PATTY SHIVERED as the blizzard winds almost lifted her off her feet. How she wished she'd never left her house!

Last night Captain Donovan had made everything sound so clear and reasonable that Patty felt dumb for not seeing things his way. He didn't seem to understand that she was just a ten-year-old kid. She had the feeling that everytime he looked at her, all he saw was her stratospheric IQ, and that made her mad. She was so many other things besides, and he'd probably never know about any of them.

Not like Murphy.

But Captain Donovan had been right about one thing: her mom had given up an awful lot to give Patty a happy life. Now her mom had a chance to be happy, herself, with Murphy O'Rourke, but that just wouldn't be possible as long as Patty was in the picture. Murphy would never stay put in Rocky Hill. He wanted to go back to London and Paris. If Patty went to that sleep-away school in Massachusetts, her mom wouldn't have to work so hard. Maybe she could even go with Murphy on one of those backpacking-through-the-Alps adventures he was always talking about.

Her mom had done so much for her. It seemed to Patty that this was the least she could do for her mom.

Patty's intention to find Captain Donovan had been good but she hadn't counted on a blizzard of such ferocity, or buses that had stopped running long before she made it to the bus stop. And she sure hadn't counted on how awfully hard it was to see where you were walking when the wind blew snow into your eyes—and the tears were flowing freely.

A vicious gust of wind-driven snow swept down on Patty and knocked her to her feet at the side of the road—what road it was, she didn't know. She struggled to get back to her feet but another blast of snow and then another made it impossible for her to regain her bearings.

"Help!" Her cry seemed tiny and lost in the scream of the storm. "Help me, please!"

Oh, Mom . . . Murphy . . . where are you?

"ANYTHING?" Murphy had to yell into the receiver to be heard over the storm howling all around the telephone booth off Route 1.

Teddy's voice sounded faint and faraway. "Nothing yet, Murph, but we've got all cars out searching. She'll turn up."

Same story from Dan Stein's local contact and from Scotty and Caroline and the guys from the rescue squad. He hesitated calling Sam but it had to be done.

"I'm heading down toward the mall," he said, trying to sound more confident than he felt. "I bet she's there doing some last-minute shopping."

He hung up before Sam had a chance to hear the fear building inside his gut. Patty wasn't shopping at the mall. The mall was closed. The roads were damn near impassable and he hadn't seen a bus in hours. Every thought he had was nightmarish.

Murphy stumbled from the telephone booth and was struggling to make his way back to his car in the blinding snowstorm when he heard a noise. He stopped, tilting his head to listen. Nothing. Must be his imagination.

"Help... please help me... Murphy..."

You're going crazy, O'Rourke. Hearing voices...

"Murphy... I'm cold..."

His entire body jerked as if he'd run headfirst into a cattle prod. His heart hammered wildly inside his chest.

"Patty!" His voice roared out above the scream of the storm. "Patty, I'm here!"

Her voice was muffled, indistinct. He called upon Boy Scout training and Army boot camp and God in heaven to help him find her. The landscape was like an Arctic tundra. Snowblind, he pushed his way toward the voice in the distance.

And then he saw it. A tiny scrap of red in the ocean of whiteness. The curly pigtails of Patricia Dean.

"Murphy," she said, running into his arms. "What took you so long?"

Rough tough Murphy O'Rourke, meanest reporter in New York, lowered his head and cried.

"Is MOM GOING to yell at me?" Patty asked as Murphy eased the Blazer onto her street.

"Probably," said Murphy, wiping sweat off his forehead with his forearm. "It won't mean a thing, though."

"It's because she loves me, right?"

"You know it, kiddo. She loves you more than anything in the world."

Patty's lips curved into a smile. "She loves you, too."

Murphy almost ran off the road. "She tell you that?"

The little girl shook her head. "She didn't have to. Some things I just know."

"Yeah, well, let's wait and see." He and Sam had been on a rocky road the past week. She may have decided life with him didn't sound like such a good idea. Not that he'd pay any attention, mind you. He intended to become part of Sam's and Patty's family and he wouldn't take no for an answer.

The street looked like a Christmas card come to life. Snow blanketed everything and continued to fall. Yet, despite the blizzard conditions, candles still burned in front of one house on the entire block. Sam's house.

Next to him Patty clasped her hands together in delight. "My candles," she said in a hushed whisper. "My Christmas Eve candles!" She looked at Murphy, and the smile she gave him was pure little girl. "I think everything's going to be okay."

SAM WAS STANDING near the Christmas tree, looking out the front window when she heard the unmistakeable sound of her Blazer plowing its way up the snowy street.

"Oh, dear God, please," she whispered, her face pressed against the icy glass as she peered through the swirling snow outside. "Please bring my little girl home." The world was no longer the safe haven of her childhood; it was rougher and more dangerous. A place where little children's faces peered from milk cartons and families prayed for a miracle.

She waited, her heart pounding violently at the base of her throat, as the sound grew closer. Her legs trembled and her hands grew colder than the falling temperature. The endless hours of waiting, of praying, of lighting the candles and hanging the stockings and pretending there would be a happy ending on this holiest of nights had taken their toll and as the familiar vehicle approached, the roaring inside her head intensified, rivaling the sound of the storm.

She knew somehow that God was listening to her prayers, that He had sent Murphy O'Rourke into their lives for a reason—to love them and protect them and share the good times and the bad. The Blazer cautiously made its way up her driveway with Murphy at the wheel. Her eyes swam with tears. The passenger seat was empty. Or was it?

"Patty!" Her daughter's name was a cry from the heart as the little girl opened the car door and jumped out. Sam raced out of the house and flew down the snowy steps.

"I'm sorry, Mommy!" Sam hugged Patty so tightly the little girl's words were muffled against Sam's sweater. "I didn't mean to make you scared."

Sam tried to sound stern but managed only to sound relieved. "Where on earth were you going, Patty? What were you trying to do?"

Patty's bright blue eyes glanced from Sam to Murphy then back again to Sam. "Captain Donovan," she said, her voice little more than a whisper. "I wanted to talk to him. I thought . . ."

Her words drifted away in the wind and Sam cupped her daughter's chin, forcing Patty to meet her eyes. "You thought what, honey?"

"You and Murphy. I thought that maybe if I went away to that school Captain Donovan talked about that you and Murphy could—"

She looked up at Murphy who was listening intently to the exchange. "There's nothing more important than you, honey. There's nothing on earth I care more about than your happiness."

"I thought maybe if I went away you wouldn't have to work so hard." Her cheeks reddened. "Maybe then you and Murphy could go anywhere you want."

Murphy crouched down near them. "Running away doesn't solve anything, Patty. You should have talked to us. Maybe we had the answer all along."

Patty's mouth dropped open. So did Sam's. *One more miracle, please, dear Lord, and I'll never bother you again . . .*

"The buses stopped running," Patty said, sniffling. "I only got halfway and then I got lost."

"Why didn't you call?" Sam asked, kissing her soundly and administering another bone-crushing hug. "Don't you know that I'm here for you no matter what?"

"I lost my money in a snowdrift," said Patty, "and then I tried to find my way back but everything looked all white and the same."

"Tell me about it," said Murphy, tugging fondly on one of Patty's braids. "If it weren't for this head of red hair, I might never have found her."

Sam looked over at Murphy, at that dear and handsome face, and saw her future reflected in his eyes. "I'll never be able to thank you," she said, wishing she knew the right words to convey the powerful rush of primal emotions taking root inside her heart. "I—"

"Mom," said Patty, once more her practical, brilliant little girl, "can we talk inside. It's *freezing* out here!"

"Come on," said Sam, smiling at her two favorite people in the world. "Let's get you guys warm."

A FEW HOURS LATER, Sam tucked the afghan around her sleeping little girl and kissed the top of her head.

"She looks like an angel, doesn't she?" She turned to Murphy who was sitting in front of the fireplace in the living room.

"You look like an angel," he said, motioning for her to sit down next to him. "I don't think I'll ever forget the way you looked when you saw Patty get out of the Blazer."

Sam snuggled up next to him and kissed him soundly. "I owe it all to you, Murphy. You saved her life."

Was she imagining it or did her hero actually blush. "I wouldn't go that far, Sam."

"I know you saved my life."

"Your life was just fine. You didn't need anyone to save you from anything."

She swallowed hard. This wasn't the time for anything less than total honesty. "You saved me from being lonely, Murphy. I didn't think I could fall in love."

He met her eyes. "Past tense?"

"Past, present and future. I love you, Murphy O'Rourke. God help me, but I do."

"I love you, Sam." Murphy's words were the first Sam heard as Christmas Day came to Rocky Hill. "I love you and I love Patty and the best present you could give me is to say yes."

"Yes," said Sam as love and happiness and hope filled her heart to overflowing. "Yes! Yes! Yes!"

He laughed and held her close. "You haven't heard the question yet."

She pulled away a fraction and looked up at him. "You're asking me to marry you, right?"

"That's right."

Her breath caught for an instant. "You won't be going overseas?"

"Not on your life."

"Your job—what will you do?"

He gave her a sheepish, but extremely self-satisfied grin. "Meet Murphy O'Rourke, managing editor of the *New York Telegram*, and stalwart citizen of Rocky Hill, New Jersey."

She laughed despite herself. "You mean, you'll be a commuter?" Dashing, dynamic Murphy O'Rourke riding New Jersey Transit!

"A commuter," he said, gathering her close to him. "Life is full of surprises."

"No more Paris nights and London weekends," she said softly. "Any regrets?"

He looked at Patty, sleeping, then met Sam's eyes. "Only that I didn't meet you a long time ago."

"We still have plenty of time, Murphy." She kissed him on the lips. "But not if you don't ask me officially."

Grinning he dropped to one knee before her. "Will you marry me, Sam?"

"Yes!" She threw herself into his arms. "I can't think of anything on earth I'd rather do."

THE SIGHT OF GROWN-UPS kissing usually made Patty giggle and look away.

But not tonight. She watched from under the afghan as her mom and her almost-dad kissed each other by the light of the fire and started to plan a lifetime of happiness for the three of them.

Two tiny packages rested under the tree, wrapped in shiny paper of gold and silver. Halves of the same heart. One inscribed "Mom." And the other inscribed "Murphy," but not for long. The day after Christmas she'd ask her mom to take her to the mall where she'd have the jeweler inscribe "Dad" right there for the whole world to see!

"You'll get your wish, Patricia," the Macy's Santa Claus had said. "I promise you!" And even though Patty was too old to believe in Saint Nick, she'd somehow known the man in red was telling the truth.

Mr. and Mrs. Murphy O'Rourke. How wonderful it sounded.

Patricia O'Rourke. How terrific it would look, written in her diary in her very best script.

The O'Rourke Family. Now that was the very best of all. Her mom had Murphy to love and Murphy had her mom, and Patty was lucky enough to have both of them as her very own parents forever and ever.

From the churches of Rocky Hill came the glorious sounds of the church bells tolling midnight as Christmas carols rang out up and down the quiet, snowy street. What a wonderful day it would be.

She sighed happily and closed her eyes. "Merry Christmas to all," she whispered as sugarplums began to dance inside her head, "and God bless us, every one!"

H A R L E Q U I N
American Romance®

A Holiday Message to my Readers....

Like everyone else I'm still searching for the perfect Christmas. While I imagined other families gathered around the hearth sipping eggnog by firelight, my family gathered by the stove arguing about the turkey. Somewhere families gathered in serenity. Somewhere, but definitely not here. As my husband says, my family is small but volatile.

Ten years ago, when I was still too young to know better, I decided to do something about it. My husband had to work a half day on Christmas and, rather than the two of us fighting the traffic into Queens just for dessert, I opted for Christmas à deux. I cleaned the house until it sparkled like the lights upon the tree. The aroma of cinnamon wafted from the kitchen. We sipped eggnog and listened to carols while I tried to ignore the pile of shiny red-and-green packages that wouldn't be delivered until the next day.

I had my peaceful Christmas. A cathedral couldn't have been more peaceful than our house that evening. No hassles. No headaches. No darned good. My husband glanced at me as we put away our dinner plates. "I don't know about you," he said, "but all this peace and quiet is depressing me."

I nodded and we grinned at each other. What I hadn't realized was that my idea of a perfect Christmas had nothing to do with real life. What makes Christmas or Chanukah perfect is being with those you love, sharing the jokes and traditions (and even the arguments!) that make your family special. Each family has its own style of celebration. Mine just happens to be louder than most.

Within ten minutes we had piled the presents and ourselves into the car and pointed it toward Queens. And, yes, we made it there in time for dessert!

May your holidays be simply perfect, this year and every year.

Barbara Bretton

CHRISTMAS IS FOR KIDS

Spend this holiday season with nine very special children. Children whose wishes come true at the magical time of Christmas.

Read American Romance's CHRISTMAS IS FOR KIDS— heartwarming holiday stories in which children bring together four couples who fall in love. Meet:

Frank, Dorcas, Kathy, Candy and Nicky—They become friends at St. Christopher's orphanage, but they really want to be adopted and become part of a real family, in #321 *A Carol Christmas* by Muriel Jensen.

Patty—She's a ten-year-old certified genius, but she wants what every little girl wishes for: a daddy of her own, in #322 *Mrs. Scrooge* by Barbara Bretton.

Amy and Flash—Their mom is about to deliver their newest sibling any day, but Christmas just isn't the same now—not without their dad. More than anything they want their family reunited for Christmas, in #323 *Dear Santa* by Margaret St. George.

Spencer—Living with his dad and grandpa in an all-male household has its advantages, but Spence wants Santa to bring him a mommy to love, in #324 *The Best Gift of All* by Andrea Davidson.

These children will win your hearts as they entice—and matchmake—the adults into a true romance. This holiday, invite them—and the four couples they bring together—into your home.

Look for all four CHRISTMAS IS FOR KIDS books available now from Harlequin American Romance. And happy holidays!

XMAS-KIDS-1R

Harlequin Superromance®

LET THE GOOD TIMES ROLL...

Add some Cajun spice to liven up your New Year's celebrations and join Superromance for a romantic tour of the rich Acadian marshlands and the legendary Louisiana bayous.

Starting in January 1990, we're launching CAJUN MELODIES, a three-book tribute to the fun-loving people who've enriched America by introducing us to crawfish étouffé and gumbo, zydeco music and the Saturday night party, the *fais-dodo*. And learn about loving, Cajun-style, as you meet the tall, dark, handsome men who win their ladies' hearts with a beautiful, haunting melody....

Book One: *Julianne's Song*, January 1990
Book Two: *Catherine's Song*, February 1990
Book Three: *Jessica's Song*, March 1990

HARLEQUIN'S "BIG WIN"
SWEEPSTAKES RULES & REGULATIONS
NO PURCHASE NECESSARY TO ENTER OR RECEIVE A PRIZE

1. To enter and join the Harlequin Reader Service, scratch off the pink metallic strips on all your BIG WIN tickets #1-#6. This will reveal the values for each sweepstakes entry number, the number of free books you will receive and your free bonus gift as part of our Reader Service. If you do not wish to take advantage of our introduction to the Harlequin Reader Service but wish to enter the Sweepstakes only, scratch off the pink metallic strips on your BIG WIN tickets #1-#4 only. To enter, return your entire sheet of tickets intact. Incomplete and/or inaccurate entries are not eligible for that section or section(s) of prizes. Not responsible for mutilated or unreadable entries or inadvertent printing errors. Mechanically reproduced entries are null and void. Be sure to also qualify for the Bonus Sweepstakes. See Rule #3 on how to enter.

2. Either way your unique Sweepstakes numbers will be compared against the list of winning numbers generated at random by the computer. In the event that all prizes are not claimed, random drawings will be held from all entries received from all presentations to award all unclaimed prizes. All cash prizes are payable in U.S. funds. This is in addition to any free, surprise or mystery gifts that might be offered. The following prizes are awarded in this sweepstakes: *Grand Prize (1) $1,000,000; First Prize (1) $35,000; Second Prize (1) $10,000; Third Prize (3) $5,000; Fourth Prize (10) $1,000; Fifth Prize (25) $500; Sixth Prize (5000)$5.

   *This Sweepstakes contains a Grand Prize offering of a $1,000,000 annuity. Winner may elect to receive $25,000 a year for 40 years without interest totalling $1,000,000 or $350,000 in one cash payment. Entrants may cancel Reader Service at any time without cost or obligation to buy (see details in center insert card).

3. Extra Bonus Prize: This presentation offers two extra bonus prizes valued at $30,000 each to be awarded in a random drawing from all entries received.

4. Versions of this Sweepstakes with different graphics will be offered in other mailings or at retail outlets by Torstar Corp. and its affiliates. This promotion is being conducted under the supervision of Marden-Kane, Inc., an independent judging organization. By entering this Sweepstakes, each entrant accepts and agrees to be bound by these rules and the decisions of the judges, which shall be final and binding. Odds of winning in the random drawing are dependent upon the total number of entries received. Taxes, if any, are the sole responsibility of the winners. Prizes are non-transferable. All entries must be received by March 31, 1990. The drawing will take place on or about April 30, 1990 at the offices of Marden-Kane, Inc., Lake Success, NY.

5. This offer is open to residents of the U.S., the United Kingdom and Canada, 18 years or older except employees of Torstar Corp., its affiliates, subsidiaries, Marden-Kane, Inc. and all other agencies and persons connected with conducting this Sweepstakes. All Federal, State and local laws apply. Void wherever prohibited or restricted by law.

6. Winners will be notified by mail and may be required to execute an affidavit of eligibility and release that must be returned within 14 days after notification. Canadian winners will be required to answer a skill-testing question. Winners consent to the use of their name, photograph and/or likeness for advertising and publicity in conjunction with this and similar promotions without additional compensation.

7. For a list of our most current major prize winners, send a stamped, self-addressed envelope to: WINNERS LIST c/o MARDEN-KANE, INC., P.O. BOX 701, SAYREVILLE, NJ 08871.

If Sweepstakes entry form is missing, please print your name and address on a 3" × 5" piece of plain paper and send to:

In the U.S.
Harlequin's "BIG WIN" Sweepstakes
901 Fuhrmann Blvd.
Box 1867
Buffalo, NY 14269-1867

In Canada
Harlequin's "BIG WIN" Sweepstakes
P.O. Box 609
Fort Erie, Ontario
L2A 5X3

LTY-H119

Indulge a Little
Give a Lot

An irresistible opportunity to pamper yourself with free gifts (plus proofs-of-purchase and postage and handling) and help raise up to $100,000.00 for **Big Brothers/Big Sisters Programs and Services** in Canada and the United States.

Each specially marked "Indulge A Little" Harlequin or Silhouette book purchased during October, November and December contains a proof-of-purchase that will enable you to qualify for luxurious gifts. And, for every specially marked book purchased during this limited time, Harlequin/Silhouette will donate 5¢ toward **Big Brothers/Big Sisters Programs and Services**, for a maximum contribution of $100,000.00.

For details on how you can indulge yourself, look for information at your favorite retail store or send a self-addressed stamped envelope to:

INDULGE A LITTLE
P.O. Box 618
Fort Erie, Ontario
L2A 5I3

ONE PROOF OF PURCHASE
To collect your free gift you must include the necessary number of proofs-of- purchase, plus postage and handling, along with the offer certificate available in retail stores or from the above address.

CHAR-3

Harlequin®/Silhouette®